WE COULD BE
BROTHERS

DERRICK BARNES

WE COULD BE BROTHERS

an imprint of Just Us Books, Inc.

Library of Congress Cataloging-in-Publication Data Available
Originally published in 2010 by Scholastic Press
ISBN 978-1-933491-24-0

10 9 8 7 6 5 4 3 2 1
Printed in the U.S.A.

The text type was set in Century Schoolbook.
The display type was set in Museo Sans.

Cover design by Ty Nowicki

For Dr. Alfred Tatum,
Associate Professor and Director of the University
of Illinois at Chicago Reading Clinic, and to all of
the young, brilliant brother authors.
Continue to speak and write unapologetically.
— DB

STRANGERS
ON
TUESDAY

2:33 P.M.
ALAIN LOCKE MIDDLE SCHOOL
THE BERMUDA HALLWAY

As soon as the bell rang, 2:30 p.m. on the dot, classroom doors swung wide open and we flew out into the hallways like we were shot from cannons. Mr. Monk's sixth-period social science class is a super-slow death. Each minute in that class feels more like five minutes. We hit up our lockers and came pouring down the main stairs from the second floor like a human waterfall flowing fast of sixth, seventh, and eighth graders spilling across the Alain Locke school crest.

Usually, I'm a part of all of that, but today was different. Today was so embarrassing, I didn't even tell my dad. I lied to him and told him that for the next three days, I'd be staying after school to work on a science fair project. Yeah, right. He'd be so disappointed if he knew the truth.

All day I thought about taking that long, dreaded stroll down the Bermuda Hallway.

On the ground floor, right next to the boys' locker room is a set of stairs that are deep, narrow, musty and hot. There have been kids who've gone down those stairs, but never came back up. It's a stupid school legend that I can't say is true or not, and I was not looking forward to finding out.

There are some kids that travel the Bermuda Hallway like they do the daily path to their own homeroom. That ain't me. I guess it'll be me for the next three days.

As soon as I walked through the raggedy, darkened doorway, the noise behind me got muffled. The laughing, the arguing, and the cussing slowly began to fade until I heard nothing but my own footsteps.

There were lights along the walls of the stairwell that flickered like somebody'd forgotten to pay the electric bill. The farther I went, the more I felt like a part of the underworld that is PSS—Post-School Suspension.

Principal Richmond refuses to waste any valuable time during a regular school day to punish students. He is the originator, the godfather, and the evil scientist behind the invention of PSS. Anytime a student gets into trouble, they'll be punished on their own time. That means sacrificing those sweet valuable hours right after school lets out. Principal Richmond knows that we'd rather be at home, playing Madden against some dude from Tokyo on PS4, smashing that leftover Pad Thai in the fridge, or just 'chillin'. Being in the basement, after school lets out, is not a good look. It's the worst. But hey, what can you do?

When I got to the bottom of the stairwell, I expected to see ashes, torn-up clothes, and the bones of kids who never made it out alive. A bunch of tubes and pipes hung above me—some metal, some plastic, some rusted. They leaked in spots and flushed, rattled, and whined in others. Soon the lights stopped flickering, and dimmed for good.

At the end of the hallway, music seeped from beneath the PSS room door. I couldn't make out what the song was. All I heard were muffled sounds. No talking, just suffocated noise and a throbbing bass line.

A sign made of a copper wired frame hung eye-level, next to the door. You can't miss it. Encased in the frame was a quote from Fredrick Douglas for all who entered the God forsaken place to read:

PEOPLE MIGHT NOT GET ALL THEY WORK
FOR IN THIS WORLD, BUT THEY MUST
CERTAINLY WORK FOR ALL THEY GET.

Derrick D. Barnes

I gave the door a tiny shove. It screeched open like an angry crow. Before I even walked inside, I heard the music crystal clear. It was "People Make the World Go 'Round" from an old-school group called the Stylistics, my dad's favorite group.

A bearded man with a large barrel-shaped gut stood up from his desk, with a weird and unexpected smile. "Come on in, son. I think you're the last one."

I stepped in, dejected and ready to face my punishment like a man.

6

2:47 P.M.
ALAIN LOCKE MIDDLE SCHOOL
THE POST-SCHOOL SUSPENSION ROOM

"Please, son, don't come in late again," said the grinning lumberjack PSS teacher. Both of his thumbs were trapped under his striped suspenders. All he needed was a pipe in his mouth. He looked like he was ready to eat a plate full of flapjacks or cut down a few trees.

"My name is Patt," he said. "*Mr.* Patt." He squeezed around his desk and stood in front of it, covering up the whole thing. Then he cleared his throat and continued. "Look, I only have one serious rule for you to follow—do the work we've provided for you. You can stay for three days or for the remainder of the month. It's all up to me."

The "work we've provided for you" was filing, stapling, and collating hundreds of papers. On top of doing this PSS thing every day after school, I'd still have to go home and do my homework. That was messed up.

Mr. Patt returned to his desk, and I settled in at a desk. There were only three others in the room. At one table was a scrawny, chicken-necked kid with thick, red hair. He was wearing his big brother's gear; everything seemed ten sizes too big, even his shoes. After finishing each stack of paper, he'd sneeze and then suck the snot back up into his nose. I thought kids stopped swallowing that stuff when they left elementary, but this guy proved me wrong. It was gross, even for a sixth grader.

Mr. Patt called over to the snot sucker, "Hey, Mackey—blow your nose, man! Nobody wants to hear that mess!"

Mackey giggled, then wiped his nose with one of his extra-large sleeves.

The only girl in the room, an eighth grader I recognized from some of my classes, named Rosilyn, dropped her stapler at her desk. She let out a heavy, drawn out sigh. Then she switched her skinny hips over to Mr. Patt's desk and snatched up a big box of Kleenex. "Dang, boy! Why you gotta be so nasty? Uuuuuuh!" Rosilyn fussed at Mackey like she was his momma.

Mr. Patt was glued to his computer. He bumped up the volume on his tablet, clicked REPEAT, and then gave the Stylistics another play. Rosilyn threw the box of tissues at Mackey. He grabbed a couple and put them in his pocket, but kept right on wiping the snot with his sleeves.

The other kid who was stuck with us in PSS also looked like an eighth grader. I didn't really know him, but I was pretty sure I'd had sixth- and seventh-grade classes with him. He sat with his back to everyone else. He didn't even pay attention to Mr. Patt when he was running down the PSS rule. He had a white set of Beats headphones, the wireless kind, glued to his ears. I could hear the bass line vibrating, as he swayed back and forth to the rhythm, mouthing lyrics like a muted MC.

He turned around once to mean-mug Rosilyn and the chicken-necked snot boy. There was a long keloid scar running from his left cheek to his chin. When I first saw him, I thought he acted like a kid who belonged in PSS—angry, a lot of attitude, and looking for a fight around every corner.

Mackey was stacking. Patt was caught up in a sudoku online tournament. Rosilyn took a break from her stapling duties. She chewed and popped her gum all the way over to my station, where I was clipping permission slips together. She worked her gum like one of those waitresses at the Waffle House. Rosilyn leaned one hand on my table and placed the other one on her pointy hip. She had on a long Locke Middle t-shirt that was tied into a big knot on one side and hung off of one shoulder. Her purple and orange tights matched our school colors, but sagged just a little around her thighs.

Still chewing, she looked me up and down and said, "What are *you* doin' down here? Ain't you in Mrs. Fariss's world lit class with me? You always sit in the front, right?" I kept paper-clipping and nodded my head yes. She emptied the paper clips from the box and scattered them all over my table. "I know you ain't trying to play me! You *can* talk, right? What's your name anyway?" Rosilyn asked.

"Robeson. My name is Robeson, okay?" I snapped at her with just a split second of eye contact.

She waved her hand in my face and snapped back at me with a grin on her face. I think she got a kick out of rubbing me the wrong way. "So you never did say why you're with us in PSS."

"It's for something stupid. I don't even belong down here."

"Yeah, none of us do. I don't care. I'll be back in here next month. I don't *eeeeven* care."

"Maybe *you* don't care, but I don't like wasting *my* time," I said.

Rosilyn rolled her eyes, took out her gum, and stuck it underneath my tabletop. She pranced over to the mean-mugging dude's station and tapped him on his shoulder. "Pacino. Pacino. PACINO CLAPTON!" He ignored her. "Let me get some of your staples, boy!"

He yanked his headphones off, turned around with his lips curled, and his fists balled up. "Don't you ever put your filthy hands on me!" he growled. "I don't want anybody to ever say they saw me close to you. You smell like old perfume and sweaty feet. Beat it, tramp! I ain't giving you nothing!"

As much attitude as Rosilyn had, I knew she had a comeback for this Pacino kid, but she kept quiet. She rolled her eyes, and slumped back to her seat, defeated.

Mackey, the snotty sixth grader, snickered. Mr. Patt never looked up from his laptop. He just mumbled, "Hey-hey-hey. Keep it down."

That was it. Nobody cared about Pacino's sharp words, which had sliced through the air, snipped Rosilyn deep, and fallen hard at her feet. Pacino's headphones fit right in between the narrow, neat lines of his cornrows like a puzzle piece. He was back to bobbing his head.

I couldn't just let his attitude slide. I really wanted to know what his problem was. Maybe I was just frustrated about being in PSS. Maybe it was stupidity. Something made me step to him.

I scooped the paper clips Rosilyn had emptied out on my table back in their box, took a hard breath, and walked over to Pacino's desk. He was taller, but definitely skinnier. I knew he was going to try to jump bad with me, but I didn't care. Somebody had to say something.

I tapped him on his shoulder. He turned around and yelled, "Look, girl, I told you to—" When he saw it was me, he stopped quick. He rested his headphones around the back of his neck, and said, "Man, . . . what you want?" He looked me up and down like I was a peon.

"I just . . . I just . . . What's up with you and Rosilyn?" I asked.

"Why? Do you want her? You can have her. She ain't nothing to me. She's been with everybody in the school anyway," he said.

"Do you know that for sure?" I asked.

"Man, . . . look at how she dresses. She's just asking for it."

"But you don't know for sure that she's been with everybody in the school, right?"

"I don't know who she messes around with, but I do know that *I* don't want her. Anyway, why do you care what I say about her?" Pacino asked. He gave me a mug so mean it would scare at least ten white women shopping on the Plaza.

I said, "I don't know her . . . not really. It just seemed jacked up that she would let you snap on her like that without apologizing. You know what I'm saying?"

Mackey finally looked up. He muttered, "Uh-oh."

Rosilyn smiled at me, and shook her head at the same time. She gave me a look like I should have kept my mouth shut.

Pacino removed his Beats from around his neck and then set them on the table. Both of his fists were clenched. He lunged at me, but I didn't move an inch. I wasn't going to let him punk me like that.

He noticed that I wasn't sweating his thug act. He said, "So what you want? I mean, you think I disrespected your girl and everything? What's up?"

I braced myself. "Would you talk to your momma or sister like that?"

"What you just say? My momma? Man, don't ask me about my momma! You don't know me like that, fool. Rosilyn knows I was just playing with her. She just needs to back up off of me," Pacino growled. Then he pushed his pointer finger smack dead between my eyes. "Look, playboy, we got two more days down here. The only reason I haven't popped you in your mouth is because I don't want to spend any more time than I have to in this hole. *That's* what's up!"

Rosilyn looked at me again and gave me the eyes of a damsel being shielded from the fiery breath of a dragon. Mackey wiped his runny nose on his other sleeve. Filthy sixth grader.

Pacino went back to mean-mugging me, but I ignored him. For some reason, because my pants weren't sagging to the floor, and I didn't keep a mean look on my face, he must've thought I was soft. He shook his head at me like I was about to be sorry that I ever opened my big mouth.

Two days left in PSS.

3:19 P.M.

I figured if I just did what I was in PSS to do—collate and clip at my desk—the time would go by faster.

I stared straight ahead at the wall. Well, not actually the wall but at an ancient Michael Jordan "Reading Is Fundamental" poster that was so old, Jordan had hair. Just when I was about to collate my last big stack, a finger as sharp as an ice pick tapped me on my shoulder. It was Pacino.

"I just don't get it," he said. "I've been over there trying to understand why you would take up for that girl when you don't even know her." Pacino stood next to me, pretending to collate so that Mr. Patt wouldn't say anything. "I mean . . . fools get knocked out for dumb stuff like that."

I was still staring straight ahead, and organizing my stacks. We were standing a couple of feet apart, but I could feel Pacino looking at me, or through me, like I was made of glass. "That's the type of thing you do for your moms or your sisters. I'm just sayin' . . . Rosilyn is used to people talking to her all crazy," he said.

"I wouldn't be used to that," I answered.

Pacino looked over toward Rosilyn. She had a pair of lava orange ear buds tucked neatly in her ears. Her hair was pulled back into a coily, springy, curly ponytail that sprayed across the top of her back like a cape. Her forehead was shiny, but her skin was perfect. A perfect brown. Sparkly lip gloss. Thin gold hoop earrings larger than the side of her face. Her long, pointy fingernails tapped on the table. Her eyes were closed, revealing her long lashes. She looked lost inside of her head, like she was in her own world. I bet it's kind of pretty in there, too.

I stopped fumbling with my papers and asked Pacino, "Whatever happened to respecting girls and all that stuff?"

"Man, first they need to earn respect. Besides, she knows I was just playin'." Pacino looked a little guilty. "And for real . . . if somebody talked bad to my moms, I'd beat them down so bad, their own folks wouldn't recognize them."

"That's what I'm talking about. I'd do the same thing." I agreed with Pacino.

"I had to check this fool last week," he said and then hopped on my desk, sat on a few leftover permission slips, and began to tell me how he landed in PSS. "This fool got all heated 'cause I scuffed his fake Timbos. I think they were Pimberlands. Pimbos." Pacino folded his arms.

"So *did* you step on his shoes? Is that how it happened?" I asked.

"I don't know. Maybe I did. Can't remember. I just stood there and waited on him to make a move, but of course he didn't."

"So who hit who first? How did the fight jump off?"

"We just stood there—well, I stood there about to readjust his jaw, but he started to back down."

"You got in trouble for that?"

"No, man! One of my boys, Steve-O, he creeped up behind me and nudged me to the side, and then threw a big bowl of chili at the dude with the fake Timbos."

"*That's* what started the fight?"

"Nope. The dude ducked and the chili hit some girl in the face. It was on then. Instant food fight."

"I heard about that food fight last week, but I didn't know who was behind it."

"Yeah, it ain't something to be proud of. He got all dirty. He had cottage cheese, beets, and that funky-smelling beef Stroganoff stuff all over his face. But me—man, I was spotless. That's why they blamed the whole thing on me," Pacino said, before he looked down at his shirt to make sure he still looked fly, or at least he thought he was fly.

"So you never did fight, huh?" I asked.

"Nope. That buster better be glad them flashlight cops grabbed me. I don't let nobody, *nobody*, jump bad with me in front of the ladies." Pacino shrugged. "Who'd *you* piss off to land down here?" he wanted to know.

I didn't have a wild story like his, but I told him anyway.

"We were taking an exam in biology and this kid that sits next to me was begging to cheat off of my paper. I kept ignoring him."

"So what did he do?" Pacino leaned off the edge of the desk.

"Man, he kept asking for answers until crazy old Mr. Crimple saw him."

"Then you and that dude started scrappin', right?"

"Nope. Mr. Crimple thought that both of us were cheating! I'm not the greatest student at Locke. God knows I wish I was, but I don't cheat. It didn't matter because Mr. Crimple sent us both to Principal Richmond's office."

"When did this happen?"

"Last Friday. It was the same day your food fight popped off."

"Richmond didn't buy your good-boy routine, did he?"

I was guessing Pacino has been in Principal Richmond's office a few dozen times.

"Nope. He gave me three days of PSS this week, and gave that other kid, Tariq, three days next week. Later, Tariq snapped on me. He said that if he saw me on the streets, he was gonna stomp me until my skull collapsed."

Pacino jumped down off of the table, rolled down his sleeves, and said, "Tariq? You mean Tariq Molten?"

"That's him. You know him?" I asked.

"That's the fool that I was about to knock out in the cafeteria! Man, he ain't nothing but talk."

"He didn't seem like all talk. This *is* the same Tariq Molten that got suspended last year for breaking some kid's nose by banging it against the lockers, right?"

"Yeah, that's him. But the dude whose nose he broke was a sixth grader. A nobody. Tariq had to do four months in juvie for that. They've got a revolving door for him down there." Pacino balled up his fist, like Tariq was in the room with us.

I said to Pacino, "It wasn't my fault. He's the one that got *me* into trouble. Now he wants to step to me? People are always trying to test you, you know?"

Pacino turned and faced the clock on the wall. "That's a shame," he mumbled.

"What's a shame?" I asked.

"Tariq knows who he can put on blast and who he better not step to." Pacino shook his head.

When the giant clock on the wall hit 3:30, Mr. Patt closed his laptop. He straightened his suspenders and stood up from his desk. "Okay, get out of here. See you tomorrow. Don't be late." He waddled out of the room. Mackey was right behind him.

Before Rosilyn left, she stopped at my desk, rolled her eyes at Pacino, and said to me, "See you tomorrow, boo." She swayed her skinny hips to the door. I was too busy thinking about Tariq's threat.

I told Pacino, "I was going to walk home, but I kind of like my skull, you know? Didn't plan on having it collapsed during this lifetime."

I checked my pockets, prayed to find some spare change to ride the Metro bus.

"Man, don't tell me you're scared of that munchkin?" Pacino laughed. "I know he's fifteen, and in the eighth grade, but you're a giant compared to him. I think he's one of those dudes with stunted growth or something. He should be taller than what he is. What are you goin' to do?"

"I don't know, I just don't want any problems. I don't have any beef with Tariq." I was hoping Pacino would help me out.

"Look, man, I got your back. I was goin' to smack the taste out of Tariq's mouth last week. He don't want no part of me!" Pacino said as he slid his Beats back into a tiny pocket in his camo backpack. "I'll come with you after school. You know, make sure he doesn't trip with you," he offered. "But first, you gotta come with me." He put his backpack over one shoulder and stood at the door, waiting for my answer.

"I mean, I'm not scared or anything. But if you want to help a brotha out, and have my back just for this week, that's cool," I answered.

"Just for this week only," Pacino agreed. "I don't like Tariq, but it ain't like me and you are 'boys' or anything. Since we're gonna be hangin' out down here till Friday, I'll do you a good deed."

I didn't really know what to say. Thanking Pacino would've made me really look like a punk. I still didn't know where we were headed, so all I said was, "Where we going?"

"Just come with me. I gotta do something I do every day. Your mommy and daddy won't miss you."

We were the last ones to walk out of the PSS room and Locke Middle for the day.

3:49 P.M.
MISS LULA'S
EAST 68TH AND CLEVELAND AVENUE

I'd never been on foot headed south of the school before. I didn't have a reason to. We walked straight down Cleveland Avenue, where there's a dip as steep as the Patriot ride at Worlds of Fun. This September afternoon was disguised as late June. I folded my jacket and slid it into my backpack. Pacino just broke out laughing after we crossed East 67th Street.

"What's so funny?" I asked.

"Man, look at you. I know what I'm gonna call you—Crease." Pacino chuckled as he pulled up his sagging jeans.

"Why Crease?"

"Look at your khakis, man. What are those, Dockers? You must have an industrial pressing machine at the crib. And that shirt looks like you showered it in starch." He kept going on about the way I dressed, how neat I was, and how "locked down" every detail about my clothes was. "Your belt is all shiny and, well, tight." Pacino stopped walking, faced me, and threw up a left-handed salute.

"Look, if your dad is anything like mine, you'd know how important it was to leave out the house looking *presentable*. He's big on that type of thing," I explained.

"Presentable for who? Squares-R-Us?" Pacino wouldn't stop cracking on my clothes.

"Yeah, well, my dad tells me and my little brother that when we leave the house, were representing our-selves and our last name. That's just the way it is. Doesn't your pops teach you that stuff too?"

He didn't answer but kept walking. We turned left on East 68th Street. I still had no idea where we were headed. We just kept walking.

When we crossed Lydia Avenue, Pacino turned to me and asked, "What part of Lee's Summit do you live in? Or maybe you got one of those old expensive cribs in Brookside."

"If I lived in Lee's Summit or Brookside, do you think I'd be going to Locke Middle?"

"I don't know. You look so out of place, dog. You look scared. You think somebody's gonna jack you or something?" Pacino cracked as we came up on about eight dudes playing basketball in the middle of the street. The hoop was made out of a milk crate nailed onto a light pole.

"We used to live downtown, but last year we moved to that new Citadel division off of 63rd Street."

"I knew it. A nice chunk of the suburbs slammed right down in the middle of the hood. It's gated, and it's guarded by the boys in blue, who're like shepherds watching over the good little Negro sheep." Pacino couldn't stop harping on how "creased" he thought I was.

"Citadel's cool. Where do you live?" I asked.

"We passed it a few blocks ago. We live in Meyer Heights, across the street from the school. We've been there for a minute—'bout ten years. There's gunplay and all, but it's home to me," said Pacino, with pride.

We kept walking. I didn't say anything. But him being from Meyer Heights explained a lot. It seemed like every other day after school, the police, an ambulance, or the fire department was over there. And at least once a month, Meyer Heights was on the news, adding to the homicide total in the city. Pacino and I only live ten minutes away from each other. Strange how people could live so close to each other but not have a lot in common.

When we stepped onto Jackson Avenue, I saw a yellow DEAD END sign. At the end of the block was one house with no neighbors on either side or directly across. There were old bikes, a swing set, and three scooters on the side of the house. In the driveway was a brand-new minivan with Jedi-black tinted windows and twenty-two-inch custom rims. There were deflated soccer balls floating in a puddle next to the curb and a homemade wooden sign, with poorly painted words, stuck into the ground that read:

WELCOME TO

MISS LULA'S HEAVENLY DAY CARE

THEY'RE ALL ANGELS WHEN THEY

PASS THROUGH MY DOOR.

6AM–6PM M–F

I didn't know what kind of circles Pacino rolled in. And now we were at some 'heavenly' day care.

"Why are we here? One of your boys sells dope out the back and uses the day care as a front?" I tried to sting Pacino for messing with me all afternoon.

Pacino barked at me, "What? Man, shut up! That's why Tariq Molten is after you now. Just follow me and keep your mouth closed when we get up in here." The front porch was completely shaded by droopy bushes.

Pacino pushed the doorbell three times and opened the screen door. He banged his knuckles against the center of the door. I didn't know what to expect, especially when a sweet and completely harmless-looking lady opened the door. She released the welcomed scent of baby powder and freshly baked oatmeal-raisin cookies. She blessed us with a warm, wide smile. Pacino immediately removed his Royals cap, then made a quick transformation into someone I hadn't seen all day.

"How's it goin', Miss Lula?" Pacino was crushing his cap with both hands like he'd just stepped into church and was trying to squash a sin.

Miss Lula spoke in a Southern hush. "Fine, just fine, Pacino. I see you've got one of your buddies with you. How you doin', baby?" Miss Lula asked me softly.

"Doing fine, ma'am." I could feel myself getting bashful. "Those cookies smell like my mom's," I said. Pacino looked over to me like he wanted to punch me in the ear.

"You kids can take some cookies with you," Miss Lula offered. "What's your name, baby?" she asked before she turned to redirect three or four small children back into their play area.

"My name is Robeson Battlefield, ma'am. I attend school with Pacino."

"Battlefield? You some kin to Reverend Battlefield over at Mount Olive? Where are your folks from?"

"My mother is from St. Louis. My dad is from Corinth, Mississippi. I don't think we're related to Reverend Battlefield. My dad would know, though."

"You kind of favor the reverend 'round the mouth and nose. That's why I'm asking. You boys have a seat." Miss Lula gestured toward her couch, which was smothered completely by plastic and needlepoint creations. Pacino grabbed me by the elbow before I could sit down.

"Not trying to be rude or anything, Miss Lula, but Robeson and I have some school stuff to do. Are the girls ready?" Pacino asked, still in church-boy-polite mode.

Before I could ask what girls he was talking about, Miss Lula called out toward the back of the house, "Lavi! Indi! Come on, girls! Your brother is here to get you."

With their matching purple jackets and teddy bear backpacks, identical twins with long bouncy curls and electric laughs came running toward Pacino. They both leaped into his arms like they hadn't seen him in months. They looked to be four or five years old.

"I didn't know you had baby sisters, man," I said to Pacino.

"There's a lot you don't know, Crease. Their school bus drops them off over here after school. Anything else you need to know?" Pacino tied the shoes of one of the twins.

"Yeah. How do you tell them apart? It's probably easy for you, since they're your little sisters, right?" I asked.

"Well, Lavender, this one right here, she laughs all the time, even when there's nothing funny. She's crazy." Pacino nudged his hands underneath Lavender's armpits, picked her up from the floor, and tickled her until her curls jiggled. "Indigo, she's a little more serious. She laughs, too, but she always wants to know the when, who, and what about stuff. That's how I tell 'em apart."

Sure enough, as soon as Pacino put Lavender down, he began to answer a bunch of kid questions from Indigo that were flung at ninety miles an hour.

"What are we having for dinner, Po?"

"Who is your friend, Po?"

"Wanna see what I did at school today, Po?"

"Is Momma gonna be at home, Po?"

Pacino answered each one as well as he could. The church boy he'd turned into for Miss Lula was now some dude from "Sesame Street." He laughed and played with Lavender and Indigo, and made sure they had everything in their backpacks.

Pacino told his sisters, "This is Robeson, but y'all can call him Crease, okay?" They looked at me with sparkling brown eyes and silly grins. "He's just hangin' out with me today. That's all. Y'all ready?"

They both screamed, "Yeeeeees!"

Miss Lula snuck off and made us four bags filled with her oatmeal-raisin cookies and bottles of 2% milk.

"Take these, boys. Have a good evening, and y'all be safe walking home." Miss Lula showed us to the door.

"Thank you, Miss Lula," Pacino said with a big smile. "My momma said she'll have the check ready for you tomorrow."

"Tell her don't worry 'bout it, baby. She can give it to me next week." Miss Lula answered with a ton of understanding in her warm voice. She gave us all a hug good-bye.

I grabbed her hand and bowed to her like she was a queen. Then I told her, "Thank you so very much for the cookies and the hospitality, Miss Lula. Really."

"Pacino, you can bring this one back anytime. A young man as respectful and nice as you are is always welcome." Miss Lula's flattery sure was sweet.

Pacino grinned at Miss Lula. But as soon as she shut the door, his smile turned off.

"What's up with you, man? I shouldn't have brought you over here. You trying to embarrass me with all of that polite charm crap?"

"Chill, Pacino. I can't help it. Polite-Charm is really my middle name. But you didn't know that." I laughed and jabbed Pacino in the arm. His expression said, *don't do that again*. "Looks like someone taught you the same thing, *Po*," I teased.

Pacino held the girls' hands as they went down the steps of Miss Lula's house. Then he turned around to me and smiled. "Good one, Crease. Good one. After I take my sisters home, I'm gonna drop you off at Tariq Molten's crib. Ha!"

When we got halfway up the block, Indigo looked up and asked Pacino the only question he didn't answer earlier, "Po, you didn't tell me so. Is Momma gonna be at home waitin' on us? Is she?"

Pacino still didn't answer. He looked down, smiled, and kept walking.

She never asked again.

4:29 P.M.
MEYER HEIGHTS
BUILDING 7, APARTMENT 717

Pacino told Lavender, "Girl, I know that you know what eight plus two is. Stop foolin' around." He sat in front of the twins at their family's tiny, round dining room table. He held up addition and subtraction flash cards. The twins answered everything Pacino threw their way.

"I know, I know. I was just being funny with you," Lavender giggled. Indigo looked at her with a straight face and took a long sip from her juice box. "It's ten," Lavender said. "And you know what else? Ten minus two is eight!"

Indigo gulped the last bit of juice, then jumped in. "And ten minus eight is two. I know that 'cause they all work together. Right, Po?"

"That's right, Indi! Give me some dap, baby girl," Pacino said, pumped up by their answering the right way. He held out his fists and the girls gave him some dap. It was a special, double-fist bump, high-five, fingering pointing thing that could have only been created by five-year-old twin girls.

Then the twins got up and squeezed their way from around the table. They picked a book of their choice from a bookcase in the hallway. "Can we go out on the stoop and read, Po? Pleeeeeease! My teacher let me pick the two new *Ruby and the Booker Boys* books!"

"I don't think so. You know what time it is," he said, and then pointed to their room. "Dinner's gonna be ready in a minute," he announced. They raced by us, grumbling like two little angry trolls.

Pacino's big-brother tutoring skills were better than mine. " 'The purpose of education is to create in a person the ability to look at the world for himself, to make his own decisions.' " I put a hand on Pacino's shoulder. I couldn't help speechifying.

"Don't touch me, man. What are you sayin'?" He shook me off like I was the flu.

"That's Baldwin. James Baldwin. My dad has that quote on a paperweight in his office at home."

"So you just go around spouting out other dude's stuff?" Pacino asked.

"You know James Baldwin, right?" I asked. He looked at me like I was crazy.

"Man, just because I live over here in the Heights don't mean I'm stupid. I just don't make it a point to memorize the words of dead writers. I've got real-life stuff to deal with, like these twins."

"I hear you," I said. Truth is, I help my little brother with his homework, but only sometimes. Pacino's responsibilities were quadruple mine. I followed him into the kitchen as he made the girls a bowl of oxtail stew that his mother had cooked before she left for work.

"You want some? Ever had hot-water cornbread? I know you're probably used to that stuff that comes from a box."

"Hey, my dad is from Mississippi. I *know* what hot-water cornbread is. Fact is, I was born in Kansas City, but my family and I spend a lot of time down south during the summer." My "country boy" comes out every now and then. I'm not new to soul food. Pacino handed me a bowl and filled it to the rim. It smelled amazing. Like it came from a gourmet restaurant. He prepared the TV trays and we all sat in the living room in front of the 55-inch flat-screen.

Pacino wanted to watch the episode of "The Walking Dead" that he recorded the night before, but the girls wanted to watch Cartoon Network. The girls won a coin toss. Thank God. I hate that zombie show. Before the TV was turned on, Pacino reminded the girls to bow their heads.

"Momma ain't here, but y'all know how we do. We gotta say grace," Pacino told the twins. They held each other's hand, closed their eyes, and bowed their little heads. So did I. Pacino prayed:

"God, thank you.

Thank you for this delicious meal that our momma has fixed for us. And thank you for Momma. She works so hard and does a great job keeping this roof over our heads, clothes on our backs, the whole nine.

Thanks for my sisters and, of course, our extra-special guest, the good brotha Crease. Amen."

We all said amen and laughed. Lavender, as usual, was cracking up the most. Indigo brought us all jelly jars filled with Sunny Delight. For dessert, Pacino went into the kitchen and brought back a bag full of LaMar's famous chocolate-covered cinnamon rolls.

After dinner, the girls asked Pacino if they could go to their room to play with their toys and watch a movie. He went in to hook up the DVD player. While he was helping the girls, I checked out the many pictures that plastered every wall in the living room.

The frames were so close together, they looked like puzzle pieces. They were all family pictures, new ones, old ones, black-and-whites of other family members. Smiling faces connected with me from every point of the room.

Pacino's mom must have left the radio on in her bedroom; it blared out a duet of songs and static from the local AM gospel station. Pacino never went in to turn it down.

No matter where I stood in that place, there was a choir belting out blessings from the bottom of their souls, and preachers praying for salvation. It seemed like God's energy floated in the apartment like the Southern aroma of that delicious oxtail stew.

In the corner behind the TV were trophies, plaques, and certificates. All school stuff. There were a few that belonged to the twins, but most of them belonged to Pacino. I saw honor roll letters, perfect 4.0 grade cards, and ribbons from academic competitions. If there was any award given away at our school for good grades, it was in this corner.

I picked up the biggest trophy that was engraved with Pacino's name. It was for a spelling bee. I was still holding the trophy when Pacino came over to where I was. "See, I knew you were the feds. Man, give me my trophy!" Pacino snarled, and then snatched the trophy from my hands.

"What are you talking about? If I had even half of this stuff, I'd be a star at my house. I barely make straight Bs, man." I went on about how cool it was that he kicked butt at school. "Look at all of these awards, man."

"Don't get it twisted, Crease. I ain't no punk or nothing. I just do these things to make my moms happy. That's all," Pacino explained as he carefully put his spelling bee trophy back in place.

"Nobody called you a punk because you make good grades. I wish I could do it more often. That's why we're at school, right?"

"Yeah. I guess so. But you know what I mean. Look, if you tell anybody, I'll put a lump on yo head the size of a camel hump!" Pacino threatened.

"Man, you're crazy! I wish I had your problem." I shook my head.

"I don't want other kids thinking I'm tryin' to be white or talkin' white like you do or calling me soft. You know?"

"No, I *don't* know. And who says white kids have a monopoly on being good students?" Pacino didn't answer. He just stood there facing his awards and trophies, not talking. "And I didn't know that using the English language like it's supposed to be used was a crime. *Talkin' white* . . . you don't know how stupid that sounds."

"Yeah. Whatever. I got a rep at that school. You don't. The only person I care about pleasing is my momma."

"Your mother looks so proud of you in that picture. What does she do for a living?" I asked.

"It depends on what day of the week. On her day shift, she's an aide at a nursing home. In the evenings, but only on Tuesdays, Thursdays, and Sundays, she works at the Target off of Wornall Road."

"Your mother works hard, huh?"

"You know it. That's why I gotta hold it down around here. I got a little hustle on the side, too. I just feel like I'm old enough to bring in some money too. You know?"

"What hustle?" I asked, then I realized I didn't really want to know. "Never mind. Besides, where is your dad? And who is that tall dude in some of these family pictures on the wall? Is that your brother?" I ran off a slew of questions just like Indigo would.

Pacino snatched one of his smaller trophies, the one closest to the TV. He held it tight and sat down on the couch, which also doubled as his bed.

"As far as my dad goes, I've never seen him. Don't really think about that too much. If you see him, tell him to holla at me," Pacino joked. "But that dude right there"—He turned around and pointed at a picture of the tall kid I asked him about—"that's my big brother, Micah; he's twenty-two. That's my boy right there." Pacino stared at the picture, and then his shoulders collapsed.

"Is he . . . I mean, is he . . . gone?" I didn't know how to ask if he was dead.

"Nope, he's still here. It's almost like he's dead, though. He's up in Leavenworth serving a five-year sentence for possession. He's in his third year now." Pacino sulked.

I tossed out more questions. "Possession of what? Crack? Weed?"

"It was possession of jelly beans and licorice, dummy." He was getting sick of my Indigo impression. "Yeah, it was crack. What else?"

"Man, I don't know a lot about that stuff."

"I know you don't. Your parents got you sheltered."

"So I'm sheltered because I don't know a lot about drugs and jail time?"

"I'm just talkin', Crease. Look at you gettin' all huffy," Pacino said. He popped me in my chest. "Wanna play some Call of Duty? I got that new Infinite Warfare." Pacino pulled out what looked like an army game from beneath the coffee table.

I didn't know anything about Call of Duty. My dad won't let me play a lot of video games because of the violence. Seems Pacino could do whatever he wanted, though. He made the grades, and there was no one at his house most of the time to tell him what to do.

"I don't think I have time to play. Let me call my dad. It's almost time for guitar practice." As soon as I mentioned guitar, I wish I hadn't. I was giving Pacino ammunition.

"The *guitar?*" He laughed so hard, it looked like it hurt. "Man, who do you think you are, one of them hard-rockin' white boys?"

"My dad supports my music, but he thinks it's just a fad. He doesn't think I'm really committed to being good."

"So what does he want you to be, a civil rights leader or something?" Pacino shook his head. He wrapped the cords around the joysticks and put the game back under the coffee table.

"Dad always wants me to volunteer with him on the weekends and stuff. He even signed me up to join a speech and debate team at our church. I just want to do my own thing sometimes." I explained.

"That is too funny. It's okay, Crease. If you wanna be a rock star, don't let me stop you. You've got your own dreams to see out," said Pacino.

I called Dad on my cell phone, and he said he'd be right over. In the short time it took for Dad to make it, Pacino ironed the twins' clothes for school the next day, washed the dishes, and vacuumed the whole apartment.

When Dad pulled up outside of Pacino's apartment building, he honked the horn to let me know he'd arrived. The window was up in the living room; I'd know Dad's three-toot honk anywhere. At the same time, there was banging at Pacino's apartment door. Pacino put the vacuum away in the hall closet, then grabbed a small leather bag from the top shelf.

"Po! Open up, man!" a deep voice yelled outside the door.

Then another voice joined in. "Yeah, Po, we're even early. Hook us up, man!"

Pacino flipped all three of the dead-bolt locks and opened the door. There were two big kids waiting. They were at least seventeen. Both of them gave me the "what's up?" nod.

Pacino snapped at the boys, who were a lot bigger than both of us. "Hey, y'all? My sisters are about to get ready for bed. Be quiet."

"All right, li'l man. Where do you want us? The usual spot?" The biggest kid removed his Chiefs skully.

"Yeah, in the bathroom." Pacino stepped to the side to let them in. I didn't know what was going on, but I decided to leave without getting deeper into his business.

When I was in the hallway outside the apartment, Pacino leaned out of the door and said, "Hey, Crease, remember when I said I have a side hustle?"

"Yeah . . ."

He reached in his little leather bag and pulled out two sets of barber clippers.

"Nobody cuts better than I do. Ten bucks a head. I'll hook your little baby 'fro up this weekend—for free! I'll get at you tomorrow, Crease." Pacino gave me a fist pound.

"Yeah, that'll be cool. See you tomorrow, man." As I walked past doors in Pacino's building, I heard wall-rattling music, a woman sobbing, gunshots and sirens from loud TVs, a baby screaming, and couples fighting.

When I walked down the steps and out of building number seven, I was a little confused. After everything that had happened that day, I honestly had no idea who the real Pacino Clapton was.

COOL
ON
WEDNESDAY

11:29 A.M.
ALAIN LOCKE MIDDLE SCHOOL
THE COURT

Tariq Molten was posted up with two of his boys outside of the Court. The Court is what we call our cafeteria because it's built like a basketball arena. Down in the center, where the game would be, is where we get our food.

Third period had just ended. I went to my locker on the first floor, the same floor the Court is on. Usually, I'm with my boy Nazr, but he was out sick. Truth is, Nazr wasn't really *sick*, but that's what he told his mom. The real story is that Nazr's cousin, Natosha from Indianapolis was in town, and she and Nazr went to a Royals game. The Royals had the Yankees in a three-game home stand. I didn't blame Nazr for being sick. When I saw Tariq and his boys, I wished I could have been "sick," too. And I would have loved to zap myself into Kauffman Stadium, far away from the Court.

Tariq and his boys were tripping kids they didn't know, and slapping girls on the butt for fun. Maybe I could cut down the side hallway and slip to the Court from the other side. When the classes from the second floor let out, I was sandwiched between seventh and sixth graders changing classes. But one of Tariq's boys spotted me. I was trapped.

He was a cocky kid with ragged cornrows. He leaned into Tariq, whispered something, then pointed in my direction. I couldn't sneak away. I had no choice but to keep walking between the seventh- and sixth-grade kids. Tariq looked dead at me and started nodding like he'd been looking for me.

Tariq's other boy, a lanky dude with long arms, was hyped. He turned and punched the lockers twice. Tariq and his boy switched from harassing girls to watching my every move. They looked ready to beat me down.

I'd never been in a real fight; I could always sense when something bad was about to happen. This was one of those times. Tariq made his right hand into a gun, pointed, aimed, and shot at me with four imaginary slugs.

I backed up like I didn't see them, turned around, and walked fast down the side hallway, where a stairwell leads up to the main office. When I looked back down the hallway, Tariq and one of his boys were chasing me. I kept my cool. I didn't run. I shut the door behind me and started to climb the stairs to the main office.

The door slammed behind me with an echo. When I started to climb the stairs, I looked up and into the face of Tariq's tall friend standing there. "Didn't think we saw you, huh?" He pounded a fist in his other hand and then folded his arms like he was getting ready to jack me up.

"I was heading up to the office," I told him as I started to step backward down the stairs.

"I don't think so. My boy Tariq's got something to holla at you about." He started coming toward me.

"Look who we have here." Tariq laughed when he came through the door at the bottom of the stairwell. His other boy, the one with the cornrows, was right behind him. I was trapped for sure. Where was Pacino when I needed him?

I turned to Tariq. "Hey, . . . what's up, man?" It's hard to fake a smile when you're not feeling it.

"What's up is that you're about to be the lead story on the five o'clock news." Tariq was wearing a black hoodie. Both of his hands were deep in his front pockets. "Lean up against that door, Chauncey," he ordered the cocky cornrow dude.

49

"This is the li'l dude you were talking about?" asked Chauncey. "You can definitely handle this one yourself, T." He leaned against the door like Tariq told him to.

"What's the problem? Is this about the test?" I set my book bag on the floor between us. "*You're* the one that got us in trouble." I said with a little bit of irritation in my voice.

The tall kid came marching down the steps. He stood in my face like he wanted to chin-check me. "He sounds like he got a beef with *you,* Tariq. How you gonna handle this? What you want me to do?"

Tariq held his hand up. "It's cool, Poke. I got this one. If you would'a just gave me the answer, fool, neither one of us would be in PSS."

"Why should I have given you the answers? If you didn't study, that's on you." I figured they were going to jump me anyway, so I said my piece loud and solid.

Poke and Chauncey made the situation worse. "Daaaaaaang!"

Poke pumped up Tariq. "You gonna let him just jump bad with you like that, T? Handle yo business, boy. Handle yo business!"

"Look at you. I can see the fear all over your face." Tariq was right up on me. But his hands were still in his pockets. I didn't know what he was about to do. Maybe I had said too much. He said, "I don't like punks with big mouths."

"Man, why are you messing with me over a test?" I asked.

"Being put in PSS got me in trouble with my P.O. One more thing and I'll probably have to—" Tariq stopped himself mid-sentence, then shoved his hands deeper into his pockets. The fact that he had a real life parole officer was proof that he was a sneeze away from being another statistic.

Chauncey told Tariq, "Quit talking to this fool. Are you gonna do it or what?" Whatever they had planned for me, it didn't look like Tariq was ready to go through with it.

"I'm about to. I'm about to. Don't rush me!" My insides were pounding. I thought for sure the school security guard, Mr. Thompson, would have kicked in the door by then. But there wasn't even a knock. Not one soul came down the stairs to break up the mess that was about to happen.

Tariq started fumbling with something in his right pocket, but he couldn't pull it out. His boys were getting jumpy. "Hurry up! Pop him!" Poke shouted.

But before any popping went off, I heard Mr. Thompson at the top of the stairs. "Who's down there? You need to be at lunch or in a classroom! Get out of here!"

"I'm gone!" Chauncey was the first to break.

Poke raced down the stairs past me. On his way out of the stairwell, he bumped me hard with his shoulder and knocked me down.

I was on the floor looking up at Tariq. He hocked a lugie and spit down on me like I was nothing. He missed my head, but a big glob of slobber splattered close to my face. "Next time, they gonna be calling yo folks to come get you from the hospital," he said before he flew out the door.

Mr. Thompson made it to the bottom of the stairs and helped me to my feet. "You all right? What are you doing here?"

"I was just . . . I was headed to the office. But I slipped and fell," I lied.

"Get to lunch or class or wherever you're supposed to be. I've got more important things to do. Go! Now!"

I didn't say anything. I just nodded yes. I was glad Mr. Thompson showed up, but not for my sake, for Tariq's. He had no idea what I was capable of.

2:51 P.M.
ALAIN LOCKE MIDDLE SCHOOL
THE POST-SCHOOL SUSPENSION ROOM

"Maaaaaan, you are crazy! Drake is the best MC on the planet. You must be smokin', boy," Pacino went off while we compared our favorite rappers.

"If a rapper has *li'l, young,* or *yung* before his name, he sucks. I'm sorry, that's just the way it is. I hate trap-music!" I was defending Common, my favorite MC.

It was twenty minutes into PSS, and neither one of us had even started on assigned work. We didn't care, and neither did Mr. Patt. He was in the semi-finals of an online sudoku tournament. Mackey had his head down at his station. Rosilyn was the only one paying attention. She was deep into our conversation. But I could tell by her nods, the way she threw her head back, and her laughs that she was on Pacino's side. Rosilyn was feeling Drake.

I had my arms folded b-boy style. "Man, you don't know what real hip-hop is, do you? I'm talking about that old-school stuff." Rosilyn covered her mouth and was cracking up. "Ever heard of Big Daddy Kane? EPMD? Eric B. & Rakim? I didn't think so." This made her laugh even more.

"I ain't never heard of them lames you just named," Pacino smirked. "If they don't get any play on the radio, on TV, or in the club, they don't matter anymore. Drake *is* hip-hop. *He's* always on the radio, not those lames that you mentioned."

"That radio garbage ain't hip-hop," I told him. "My dad has all of his old hip-hop tapes and CDs. I know what's up."

"What does your pops know about hip-hop?" Pacino asked.

"Enough. He's a music professor at U. of Missouri KC. He teaches a music history course that's all about appreciating all types of music. Plus, he ain't that old, man. The rappers he listened to talked about real stuff."

"Real stuff like what? If I want to hear some preachin', I'll go to church. It's always been about bangin' beats." Pacino stood up and started to count down on his left hand. Rosilyn jumped all on his team. She testified and waved her hands like one of the old ladies on the motherboard.

"Yep. Tight beats," she agreed.

"Money . . ." Pacino continued.

"It's always about the *money*, boy," Rosilyn piggybacked.

Pacino kept it going. "The jewelry. The gear."

"Oh yeah. We stay laced in nice clothes and diamonds, baby." Rosilyn was on her feet, dancing around.

"And of course, it's gonna always be about the young ladies," Pacino bragged with his arms folded. He shot me a b-boy stance. "And my nig—" He stopped himself before saying the whole *N* word, giving me a weak b-boy stance.

I shook my head. "See, there you go again. That's why I don't listen to a lot of that radio crap. The words that they use to describe us just ain't cool, especially the *N* word."

Rosilyn and Pacino looked at each other, and then said at the same time, "What *N* word? Nig—?"

"Yeah, yeah, yeah." I stopped them before they could use that word on me. "That's the one. Calling each other the *N* word just ain't cool."

"Says who?" Rosilyn laughed and then gave Pacino some dap. They were both cracking up, but I was serious.

"It's just not a word I grew up hearing my dad use around my house," I explained. "Y'all just throw it around like it's no big deal."

55

Rosilyn put a hand on my shoulder, and popped her gum. "It ain't a big deal, Robeson. You know your name. If I call you 'my nig,' that's something good, boo." She winked at me and smiled through lips caked with sparkly gloss.

"It's *not* a good thing, Rosilyn. I hate to hear that word and I don't like it when somebody says it to me. It's not something I want to be called." She shook her head like she was trying to understand where I was coming from.

"Crease, you're crazy. What should I say if I see you in the hallway?" The b-boy smirk had not left Pacino's face. "I know," he said, "how about brother?" He held out his fist to give me a pound. "What's good, *brotha?*"

I pounded him back even though I knew he was playing. "Brother sounds a lot better."

Pacino looked at me like he couldn't care less. "Whatever, *brotha*. That just ain't the way I get down. But if you want me to call you brotha, I will. Nobody will believe we're really brothas anyway."

"Why's that, Pacino?" Rosilyn asked.

"Look at how ugly Crease is. Besides, I'm the finest nigg—I mean *brotha* at this school."

We all laughed.

Mr. Patt was still locked on sudoku. He pumped his fist and yelled out, "Got 'em! I'm headed to the finals, baby!" We could have walked out of PSS and he wouldn't have noticed.

"I understand you, Robeson." Rosilyn grinned. "And I think you look pretty good. You aiight, boo. Plus your daddy sounds like a good man. You talk about him every day."

Pacino jumped in. "Don't he? Can't you think for yourself, boy?"

"My father teaches me a lot of stuff. Nothing wrong with that," I said.

"I'm just frontin'," Pacino said. "Your pops sounds cool. Matter of fact, I wanna meet him, 'cause I feel like I already know him."

"You're serious?" I asked. "I mean . . . he might pick me up tomorrow." At first I thought Pacino was just joking, but something sad in his eyes told me he wasn't.

"How about today, Crease? I had you all up in my spot yesterday, around my baby sisters, and even gave yo sorry butt some of my momma's oxtail stew. Today it's your turn, brotha!" Pacino had invited himself over before I'd even thought about it. He did have a point. How could I say no?

"Sure, yeah, I guess so," I said. "What about your sisters? Don't you have to pick them up today?"

"Nope. My momma is off this evening. I wanna see how the good side lives. I gotta meet the famous Battlefield clan. Y'all probably live like a TV family or something."

"TV family? Come on, man. We're just regular folks. My mother is cool. My little brother is cool. My father, my sister in college—we're all just regular."

Pacino balled up an old piece of paper and threw it at me. Rosilyn caught the ball before it hit me in my face. "Yeah, okay. Whatever, Crease," Pacino said.

Rosilyn leaned closer to me, smelling like sweet-pink bubble gum and hair gel. "I got you, Robeson. If he can come over today to meet your daddy and stuff, how about you have me over tomorrow to meet yo momma?" she whispered.

Rosilyn was inches away from plastering my cheeks with her sparkly lip gloss. I knew it was coming. I did.

"I knew it, I knew it!" Pacino shouted. "I knew you liked her, Crease."

And I sure couldn't figure out what to expect by bringing Pacino Clapton to my house.

3:42 P.M.
THE METRO BUS
63RD STREET WEST ROUTE

"Dummy, you know we can't use those anymore." Pacino laughed at me as he snatched the two bus transfers I had in my hand. He balled the transfers, and then threw them in my face. "These were from two weeks ago. Transfers expire in hours." I never really take the Metro bus. My dad picks me up and drops me off.

"I don't have any change on me. Do you?" I looked over Pacino's shoulder and saw the 63rd Street westbound coming fast from three blocks away.

"Do *I* have any money? You know I keep some paper on me, boy." Pacino pulled out a stack of tens, fives, and a few twenties. He handed me five ones like it was nothing, and then started to sing in a high-pitched voice, *"I'm a hustla, baby!"*

"All of that is haircut money?" I asked.

"Haircut-hustle money. The light bill ain't gonna pay itself." Pacino folded his money like it was a napkin, then slid it back in his pocket.

"You pay your family's electric bill?"

"Yeah, sometimes. Whatever my momma needs, I try to make it happen, you know?"

I nodded, but I didn't really know what it was like to pay bills for a family. I got an allowance for doing stuff around the house, but that money was mine to keep.

The bus came to a whistling stop. The bus driver looked tired. Her dreary eyes were focused straight ahead. She blinked a few times, then adjusted her seat belt. There was an old lady sitting in the front with purple-gray hair, and an even older man in a wheelchair sitting close to the door near the back.

Pacino got on before I did, put money in the fare box, and then went way to the back. I paid and sat somewhere in the middle of the bus.

"Crease! Why are you way up there, square?" Pacino yelled out. He leaned against his window, put his headphones on, and then stared out.

I got up from my seat and walked back to sit with Pacino.

"So what do you know about Tariq Molten?"

Pacino answered. "Why? Why you do you care?"

"I don't know. Just asking." I didn't want to tell him about Tariq and his boys almost jumping me on the stairs. He already thought I was a chump.

Pacino slid his headphones down around his neck. "Tariq's momma is an alcoholic. He's had about ten step-daddies, and I hear that almost all of them whooped his butt on the daily. He used to come to school with busted lips and black eyes." When we hit a red light, Pacino stared out the window on his side of the bus. "Tariq ran away from home about three years ago, and goes in and out of different group homes."

"Doesn't he have other family members?"

"Yeah, I guess so. Every now and then, his grandma will come get him, I hear. But then he'll do something stupid again and end up right back in trouble. I think even his granny has given up on him."

"Man, I didn't know all that."

"Come on now, Crease." Pacino shrugged.

"What? All I said was Tariq's got it bad."

"He's got it bad? Everybody's got it bad but you. Now you feeling sorry for this fool?" Pacino put his headphones back in and turned his head away from me. I went back to my old seat farther up.

The closer we got to our stop, the better things looked out the bus windows. In my subdivision, the

Citadel, houses were big, roofs were wide and new, and lawns were as green as the turf out at Arrowhead Stadium. Pacino picked up on it right away.

"Mansions in the hood," he said. "And what's so cool is, one of them belongs to you!" Pacino cheered. "Like I said, you got it good, Crease."

"I just live here," I said. "My dad reminds us that nothing we have came free. God can take it away just like that."

"Whatever, Crease. I don't know which one of those joints you live in, but if it was me, I'd throw a party up in that piece every weekend, with all my boys and music, and with *ladies* everywhere."

"Citadel!" announced the bus driver. I grabbed my stuff and stepped off the bus at the front. I thought Pacino was behind me, but he'd already slipped out the bus's back door. He was helping the bus driver lower the elderly man in the wheelchair onto the sidewalk.

"How's that? You cool?" Pacino asked the man as he rolled him over to the sidewalk.

"That'll do just fine. Thank you, young brotha." The man was all smiles.

We watched him nudge the little lever that controlled his motorized wheelchair and cross the street toward Harold Pener Men's Wear. "Pacino, man, that was cool."

"Crease, that ain't nothing new for me. I'm always willing to help my fellow *brotha*, even an *old* brotha. You haven't figured me out yet?"

I gave Pacino the brother-to-brother up-nod. Together we walked down the hill that leads to my house.

4:19 P.M.
6288 CITADEL CIRCLE
BATTLEFIELD RESIDENCE

One of the three garage doors was wide open. My mom's new Mercedes was inside; Dad's Porsche Panamera was parked in front of the middle door. I knew the third slot in the garage was empty. My sister usually parks there when she comes home over her breaks from college.

"This is *sweet*, Crease. You got a good life, and I haven't even seen the whole house yet." Pacino dropped his bag on the floor and looked around like he was in the Taj Mahal. "There's gotta be at least three bedrooms, right? Four?"

"Five."

"Five bedrooms? This is a hotel, man. I gotta see your room. You probably have a two-lane bowling alley up there."

"Man, just come in." I triggered the sensor to close the garage door.

When we got inside the house, we stepped into my dad's latest and biggest home-improvement project— a finished entertainment theater that Dad and a couple of his construction friends finished a couple of weeks ago. The carpet is plush, and the brown leather love seats make us feel like we're at a big Hollywood private viewing for a new film. The best part, other than the surround-sound, is the ninety-five-inch projector screen and framed movie posters.

Pacino was all eyes. "I knew Battlefield sounded like a name for rich folks. Your parents are paid."

"Look, it's no big deal."

Pacino was all over it. "I'll be coming to watch all of the Chiefs games for the rest of the season in this no-big-deal."

There was a stack of big boxes from the entertainment equipment that formed an aisle leading to the love seats. Carmichael, my little brother, jumped from behind one of the boxes, wearing his Darth Vader mask and holding a toy lightsaber. He let out what was supposed to be a scary "GRRRRRRRRRRR!!!"

Pacino jumped back.

"Pacino, this is my little brother, Carmichael. He's eight."

"I'm almost nine!"

"So what. You're eight now," I said. I flipped his mask up on his forehead and untangled his cape.

Pacino was laughing. "Carmichael, huh? How about I just call you Money Mike?" Pacino had his hand out, waiting for my little brother to give him some dap. Carmichael left him hanging.

"I would shake your hand . . . but I don't think so." Carmichael pulled his mask back down over his face, held his lightsaber up, and posed like a Jedi knight.

"Man," Pacino said. "I can't believe I just got dissed by an eight-year-old. What's up with your little brother, Crease?"

"You gotta excuse him," I apologized. "He's nothing like me."

"You got that right," Carmichael said. He flipped his mask back up on his forehead, turned toward Pacino, and preached, "Hey, if we're going to be cool, you can at least respect a Black man enough to call him his real name, right?"

Pacino couldn't stop laughing. "That's cool, li'l dude. Sorry 'bout that. Carmichael, right?" Pacino put out his hand again.

"Carmichael Battlefield. The one and only. Nice to meet you, my brotha," he said. They finally shook hands. "Are you eating with us, Pacino?" Carmichael asked.

Pacino looked at me and shrugged.

"Am I, Crease? It sure smells fire, whatever it is." The smell of my mom's cooking floated from the kitchen, down the stairs, around a corner, and danced right into our noses.

"I *think* my mom will be cool with you staying for dinner," I answered. Not really sure.

Carmichael jumped in. "We always welcome guests, Robeson. You know that."

He fixed his mask and took off running with his red cape flapping. "I'll run up to ask her to set another place at the table."

"Wait a minute, Carmichael!" I called out. "What about the report you turned in Monday? Did you get it back today?"

Carmichael hit the brakes, pulled his mask off again, turned, and said, "Sure did. Got a hundred percent, Robeson. Ms. Basil loved it!"

"Hey, Carmichael, didn't I tell you that Steve Biko would be a good choice?" I said.

"You sure did. Thanks for the tip, Robeson. Gotta go." He took off running again.

"You help your li'l brother with his schoolwork, too?" Pacino asked.

"I just gave him the idea. My dad usually helps him with the nitty-gritty day-to-day homework. I'm not the brainiac that you are, geek," I joked with Pacino.

Pacino faked a threat with his palm stiff in midair, ready to strike. "Man, I'll smack you in the back of the neck. I ain't no brainiac geek, man."

4:44 P.M.
BATTLEFIELD RESIDENCE
THE KITCHEN

The smell of my mom's lasagna pulled us up the stairs.

Pacino and I went into the kitchen like hungry lasagna zombies. "I know I'm staying now. Your momma must be a chef."

Mom was standing in front of the sink with one hand on a hip and the other holding her phone against her shoulder. She was looking out over our backyard, talking to her friend.

"Okay . . . okay, girl. It's time for dinner . . . yeah. Robeson brought one of his friends home . . . I'll see you at the airport tonight, Patty. Bye." Mom wiped her hands on a dish towel, turned around, and smiled at Pacino and me.

"Why are you going to the airport tonight?" I asked.

"Anybody ever told you that it's bad manners to eavesdrop?"

"Sorry. . . . So where are you going?"

"I'm going to the entrepreneur's conference in Maryland. You forgot, old man?"

Mom is always traveling on business. I forget about her trips lots of times. She could tell by the lost look on my face that this was one of those times.

She pinched me on the cheek and then gave me a hug and kiss. She nodded to Pacino. "Who is this handsome friend of yours?" Pacino shoved his hands into his pockets. For the first time ever, he looked nervous.

"Mom, this is Pacino," I said. "How are you doin', ma'am? I'm Pacino Clapton." He transformed again into the nice dude he was over at Miss Lula's place. Like Miss Lula, my mom eats that stuff up.

"Nice to meet you. Are you an eighth grader as well?" Mom straightened out her Florida A&M t-shirt. She never misses an opportunity to proudly display the loud orange-and-green seal of her alma mater.

"Yes, ma'am, eighth."

My mom kept smiling, but she was checking out Pacino's rough clothes and hair. That's a skill Mom has. She makes you feel comfortable, but at the same time she's looking you over to see what you're about.

"And I'm sure you're one of the better students at Locke. Am I right, Pacino?" Mom asked.

"You know it, Mrs. Battlefield. I hit the books hard. I keep a 3.65 GPA or above." The trophies and stuff at his house said Pacino was telling no lie.

"Excellent, Pacino," Mom said. "Robeson does his best. Right, baby? In fact, every time he brings home a good grade, we try to do something special for him to keep him motivated."

"Come on, Mom," I said. "Look, my grades are improving."

"Whatever you say, Robeson." Pacino patted me on my head like I was a stray mutt or something.

"Well, Pacino, if you can just make sure Robeson stays on the right track academically, you're welcome over here anytime for dinner," Mom said.

"Yes, ma'am."

Finally, Mom said, "By the time you boys come back from washing your hands, the food should be on the table. Hurry now."

5:03 P.M.
BATTLEFIELD RESIDENCE
THE OFFICE

I let Pacino use the bathroom first, the one across the hall from my father's office. Pacino was taking forever, and I started to do the I-have-to-pee dance.

"Man, hurry up in there!" I banged on the door.

Dad's office door was closed, but I could hear his fingers tap-dancing on his computer keyboard and soft music escaping from beneath the door.

Pacino finally came out. "What's wrong with you, Crease? Can't a *brotha* use it in peace?" He'd managed to yank his pants up a bit, and it looked like he'd wetted his face.

While I was washing my hands, I heard Dad open his office door. He introduced himself to Pacino. "Come on in, young man. You like Bach's music?"

"Is that what you're listening to . . . sir? You're into that stuff?" I heard Pacino ask.

"Music of all sorts is what I do; I'm a student of every genre of music, son," Dad said.

"This is some I could do without. Seems cold as ice."

That's when I came out of the bathroom as fast as I could. Nobody disses Dad's music.

Pacino was thumbing through a gigantic, dark brown, leather-bound hunk of pages covering the history of classical music. Dad had about a little over twenty wooden pedestals and shelves stacked with old relics like albums, cassette tapes, and CDs positioned around his office. Each one showcased a "bible" or collective history of every major music genre, even one on hip-hop.

Even though Dad and Pacino had met, I started to introduce them. "This is Pacino, Dad."

"We've already met, and I know this man can speak for himself. I've heard him." Now Dad was giving Pacino the eye, checking out his clothes. Pacino was ready to defend. Before Dad could even ask, he was explaining himself.

"It's Pacino, like the actor. You know . . . Scarface?" Pacino explained, easing his way over to Dad's rock 'n' roll albums.

Dad pulled his favorite Jimi Hendrix and showed it to Pacino. He was playing it cool, but I could tell he was about to do some digging.

"Pacino, an intriguing name. Are your parents Italian?"

"No, sir, they just thought the name sounded cool," Pacino said, still thumbing through the records.

Pacino walked over to the jazz section and started flipping.

Dad handed him a Miles Davis. "Take it, Pacino. There's no ice in Miles."

Pacino gave Dad an up-nod. He was slow to take the CD. "I can borrow it? For real?" He was so excited, it seemed like Dad was letting him hold on to an actual trumpet from Mr. Davis himself.

"For real," Dad said.

Right then, Carmichael stormed in. "Dinner!" he shouted.

"Let's grub," I said.

Pacino gave one swift yank to his pants. His jeans had begun to sag way down.

We turned to leave the office, but Dad stopped us. "Robeson, before you get to the dining room, get your friend a belt." Pacino looked busted. Dad said, "If you're going to dine with us, you gotta come to the table correct."

"What? Why, Dad? I mean . . . he's okay."

"Its okay, Mr. Battlefield. I'll just pull 'em up. I always wear my gear like this." Pacino was trying to be cool, but the pants were droopy and looked stupid.

"Not good enough, Pacino." Dad took off his glasses, clipped them in his collar. "What if I wore my pants like that? Do you think my students would listen to me?"

Pacino shrugged. "I don't . . . well, . . . maybe they . . ."

"No, they wouldn't. They wouldn't respect me as a teacher or as a man." Dad was gearing up to lecture. He unclipped his glasses, cleaned them off with a suede rag that he keeps in his pocket, and then slid them back on his face.

"You're probably right. I don't know," Pacino mumbled.

I really felt for Pacino. Dad could get preachy. "Dad, it's okay. Really." But my pops wasn't buying it.

"Your last name is Clapton, right?"

"Yes, sir." Pacino answered like a little kid.

"That name means something to your folks, and it should mean something to you." Dad tapped Pacino on the chest twice. "No real man walks out of the house looking like a clown. You gotta know that. If for nobody else, wear the belt for *you*, Clapton."

Bam! Dad was laying it down hard.

Pacino looked like he wanted to defend his "droopy drawers," but the brother was dried up for a comeback. He nodded once, then managed to say, "You're right,

Mr. Battlefield. This is your house. I respect it and you." Then he turned to me. "Come on, man, let's go get that belt. I'm starving."

"Good deal. Thanks for understanding, young brotha," Dad said to Pacino. As we turned to walk out the door, Dad landed a hand on Pacino's shoulder. "Hey, man, just because you wear a belt doesn't mean your pants need to be pulled up to your chest. You know what I'm saying?"

Dad could always lighten a blow after he'd delivered it. He'd put Pacino at ease.

Pacino laughed, "Yeah, I got it."

"You don't have to be a square, a chump, or whatever term you guys use these days. You can still look decent with a belt on."

"I guess . . . I mean yeah, okay." Pacino was out of the office fast, holding tight to his Miles Davis CD.

5:19 P.M.
BATTLEFIELD RESIDENCE
THE DINING ROOM
BLESSING THE MEAL

"It's about time!" When we got to the dining room, Carmichael was at the table, ready to grub.

Mom noticed the belt on Pacino's pants. She looked at Dad, then me. "You can sit next to Robeson, Pacino. Carmichael will sit next to me tonight."

Pacino slid onto the seat next to Robeson. He kept shifting his seat, uneasy. Mom asked Dad to bless the food. She held Dad's hand, then mine. Pacino slid his hands in his pockets.

"Come on, man, reach," Carmichael said as he stretched across the table as much as he could to catch Pacino's hand.

Pacino was slow to take one hand out of his pocket, but he reached out to Carmichael. He took his other hand out of his pocket and grabbed my hand fast. He wouldn't look at me, but his grip was firm.

"Everything smells delicious, Celeste," Dad complimented my mom's cooking skills.

Dad bowed his head and began to pray over the food, like he does every night:

"Thank you for this blessed evening. I thank you for my beautiful, loving wife, Nina, who prepared this magnificent meal. Thank you for my children: Carmichael, Robeson, and Laila. And thank you, Lord, for the presence of our guest, Pacino Clapton.

Walk with us and guide our steps."

Pacino was the first to say, "Amen."

After dinner I took Pacino upstairs to show him my room before he went home. Dad said that he would give Pacino a ride. "Well, . . . here it is. It's nothing special, but it's my spot; this is where the magic happens," I said.

Pacino was back to acting like he always did—giving me a hard time about my style. "What magic? Ironing your khakis? Twiddling your thumbs? Strumming your guitar? Magic. Yeah, right." He looked around, dropped his bag on the floor, and then hit me with a face full of disappointment.

There's no TV in my room, so no video games either. But everything was where it was supposed to be. The bed was made perfectly: no lumps, no bumps, and no lines. The floor was clean: no shoes, no paper, no dirty underwear, and no dust. My guitar was propped up on a stand.

"Crease, I could have had dinner up here—on the floor! Brother, you are a neat freak!" Pacino laughed.

He looked around and noticed how naked my walls were. The only thing hanging up was a big poster of the Last Supper over my bed. In this one, Jesus is black, and his disciples are people like Marcus Garvey, Mary McLeod Bethune, Malcolm X, Booker T. Washington, and Martin Luther King, Jr.

"Now, that's cool. A black Jesus—I'm feeling that one."

I showed Pacino my autograph collection from NFL players.

"My dad knows a couple of them, like Justin Houston and Travis Kelce."

Pacino stared at the collection like he was looking at a suitcase of dollar bills. "This is better than black Jesus. Why don't you get one of these big football dudes to take out Tariq Molten for you?" He was running his finger over one of the autographs. "You never know, the next time Tariq and his boys run up on you, you might not be so lucky to get away."

"How'd you find that out?" Pacino knew that I almost got jumped earlier in the day?

"There ain't much that goes on at school that I don't know about. Anyway, kids are calling you a punk, man. Everybody."

"I don't care. The people that you're talking about, I probably don't even know them."

"You better start to care, Crease. Tariq don't play. I wish I could've been there to help," Pacino offered with a shrug. "I can't be around every waking moment, brotha."

"Meaning?" I asked.

"Meaning that Tariq will go all out. He's street. You ain't even. That's real." Pacino tried to explain to me the best way to get out of a Tariq Molten beatdown. "Don't even try to fight back. Just take his little weak punches, go down, and keep it movin'."

It was time I showed Pacino what I was really about.

"Pacino, come over here and check this out." We stepped over to my walk-in closet. I swung open both doors like we were entering a secret bank safe. On the left side hung all of my clothes.

"Your Poindexter-wardrobe? That's what you wanted to show me?" Pacino asked. I didn't answer. I just turned on the closet light and exposed my biggest secret, a secret that no one at my school knew.

"Crease, what is all of this?" Pacino's face was spray-painted with shock.

"That one there, the silver one, I won last month. First place in the annual Midwestern Martial Arts Conference and Competition." The entire right side of my closet was lined with trophies ranging from statuettes to one as tall as me.

"Let me get this right—you won these? I mean, they look like karate trophies. I must be trippin'!" Pacino held a trophy in each hand. "Man, there has to be almost thirty awards here. How'd you do it, Crease?"

"It's called kyokushin and it's built on the martial arts principles of self-improvement, discipline, and hard training."

Pacino, still in awe of all of the hardware I had on display, put the two trophies down and read my name on a bigger one, a huge bowl.

"*Kyo*-what? Is that like karate?" he asked.

"It's a sparring version. I've been training and competing ever since I was six."

"Crease, man, you are a secretive dude. Have you ever knocked somebody out, broke some bones, or got chin-checked yourself?"

"That's not really what kyokushin is about. I didn't get into it to see how many people I could hurt," I answered. "It's about soundness of mind, not kicking butts."

"Dang, Crease! I would have never guessed!"

Pacino bumped his shoulder to mine. "So if you're so good, how come you need me to watch your back?

Tariq Molten wouldn't step to you if he knew what kind of skills you had. You could cripple that boy."

"I've never had a *real-real* fight in my life. I compete for the sport, the competition. Tariq seems like he's for real. I know he or one of his boys probably carries a gun, or a knife, or brass knuckles or something."

"Brass knuckles? Man what you think this is *Grease? West Side Story?*" Pacino cracked up.

"What do you know about those movies?" I asked.

"You ain't the only one with Netflix, fool." I laughed.

"Okay, well maybe not brass knuckles, but you know what I mean. I know *you* know what I mean. Dudes like Tariq and his boys, dudes like . . . " I paused.

"Go ahead, say it—thugged-out delinquents that keep a nine in their backpacks? Is that what you mean? Dudes like me, right?" Pacino asked.

"Yeah, I guess so. Tariq seems like the kind of dude that could get a gun real easy."

"Hey," Pacino said. "Why don't you show me some of those deadly, nose-busting, bone-breaking kyo-whatever moves that you know." Pacino made some fake karate moves. "You may not want to bust Tariq up, but I ain't got no problems doin' him in. You know what I mean?"

"I don't want to hurt Tariq or anyone. He's got enough problems. Ever heard of just avoiding a fight?" I asked.

"Yeah, I heard of it. And I'm not talkin' about that stuff that happened in the Court. I'm talkin' about a real fight. The last time I tried to 'avoid' a fight, I was left with blood on my face." Pacino pointed to the scar on his cheek. "If I were you, I'd handle Tariq before he handles you."

"You're *not* me. The martial arts are serious, plus, you need to learn something about self-control."

"Self-control? I'll control this fist up side his head and put him to sleep for good."

"There you go again, Pacino. That's what I'm saying. Everything has to come down to somebody getting hurt. My dad says prisons and graveyards are running over with brothas, young and old. And he says that we don't need to add to that population."

"There *you* go, quoting your dad again. You saw where I live. That's how you have to think or else you'll get your butt beat on the daily." Pacino laid it down seriously. "Tell me, Crease, do you have one original thought? Your pops has programmed you. You're like a puppet around that man."

Pacino could diss me, but not my dad. "A puppet? He's my dad, man. At least he makes sense. Let's say you hurt Tariq or keep thinking that everything has to be handled by fighting and stuff, then you'll be sharing a jail cell with your dumb brother. Is that what you want? Your mother will have two boys in the joint. You think that will make her happy?"

Pacino's jaw got tight. "See, you didn't even have to mention that." The joking, talks of karate lessons, and taking care of Tariq Molten had slammed into a stone wall. He wasn't smiling anymore. "Why'd you have to put my brother in this?"

"Because this is about brothers. It's about you and me. You can't go around thinking you're tougher than everybody else, Pacino. My dad—" I began, before Pacino cut me off.

"*Yo daddy. Yo daddy. Yo daddy.* Man, forget you and your daddy. You think you're better than me 'cause you live over here?" he spat. "You think you're better than me because your folks got a little money, and you don't have to worry about bullets flying through your bedroom walls at night, right?"

"No, man. I never said that. I was just—"

"Come on, Crease, you thought I was just the type of dude that wouldn't mind getting shot, or getting into a fight for somebody. You think your life means more to you than mine does to me?"

"The way you talk sometimes, it doesn't seem like you care about anybody but yourself."

"It's like that, right?" he asked before he snatched his bag from the floor and made his way toward the door. "Let's see how you do without me. I hope they catch up with you. You think they look at you like a brother, *brotha*? I'll tell your pops that I'm ready to bounce. I'm out."

Pacino threw me the illest mean-mug ever made by a human face. He charged out of my room and never looked back.

BOYS
ON
THURSDAY

10:27 A.M.
ALAIN LOCKE MIDDLE SCHOOL
THE AUDITORIUM

"One more time, students. Let's stand up and give a warmer and *more* enthusiastic round of applause for Dr. McKinney and his all-star staff of award winning, traveled archeologists." Principal Richmond's shadow draped over the first twenty rows of the auditorium. His voice was ten-ton heavy and his suit was wide, black, and serious.

Even though all of us were bored out of our domes, we stood up and clapped a little bit harder. Principal Richmond scares most of the students at Locke, but not me. He reminds me a lot of my dad.

That Dr. McKinney guy was kind of a big deal. He was a scientist, an artifacts collector, and a marine biologist. He'd discovered a sunken slave ship at the bottom of the Atlantic Ocean. He and his crew were showing us some of the valuable remains they found.

It was cool to me, but most of the seventh and eighth graders in the auditorium were ready to leave. It was lunchtime for some, and third period for others.

Principal Richmond sent out another wave of instructions. "I trust that all of you are responsible enough to go wherever it is that you belong. If any of you are caught somewhere you're not supposed to be, you'll have to answer to me. That's all I'm going to say. Good afternoon."

He dismissed us, and we all took off in our own directions like shattered glass. During the crowds and craziness, I ducked off into an aisle to let the bum-rushing stream of chaos pass me up. Way at the end of the line was Pacino. He saw me, too. He came up and gave me a pound. It was like last night never happened.

"My man, Crease. What's up, Kung Fu Joe?" He gave me another pound and chopped me with his other hand across the back.

"Nothing much. You?"

Pacino was wearing the belt I'd given him. His pants were up at his waist, looking decent, not droopy.

"Hey," he said, "last night I was trippin', aiight."

I adjusted my backpack. "Yeah, cool. No big deal, man." I was kinda out of line when I mentioned his brother. "Carmichael wondered why you left so fast. He wanted to show you his spelling test scores."

"Tell the little man I said what's up. Your little brother is about ten times as cool as you are." Pacino laughed and attempted to give me some more dap. I left him hanging and shoved him a little.

The hallway was noisy, and kids were shoving.

Pacino looked around. In a hush, he said, "I gotta go to the senior building and start taking Advanced Placement math class." Then he shrugged and looked at me like there was something really wrong.

"Man, don't you know how crazy that is? An eighth grader taking an AP class? That's bananas, bro!" I was trying to hide the envy in my voice. My mother would throw a parade if I told her I was taking a class with high school kids.

"You know I'm brilliant, baby. But that's between us, cool?"

"Cool." I gave him a jab to the gut. "I'm headed to African American history."

Pacino pulled me out of the way so other kids could pass us. "Wherever you go, watch your back. I heard something about ya boy Tariq." He was looking me dead in my eyes, completely serious.

"What did you hear? Tell me, man." The auditorium was beginning to empty, but I wasn't going to move until Pacino told me what he'd heard.

"A girl that rides the bus with one of them dudes that tried to jump you with Tariq said that he was strapped today. I think they said he had a thirty-eight, a nine or something. I don't know."

"Serious? I mean, you think I should tell somebody? You think he's gonna try something with me?" My neck started to get warm. Pacino looked worried.

"Calm down, Crease. Tariq might have something, he might not. But what you can't do is tell on him. If he's got his eyes on you, he's got his eyes on you. That's all there is to it."

"Look, I don't want to get shot today, or tomorrow, or the day after that." Now my whole face was hot.

"What did I tell you on Tuesday, huh? Didn't I say I had your back?" He stood over me with a hand on my shoulder, like a big brother.

"Yeah, but what about all of that stuff you said yesterday about me being on my own?"

"Look, that's squashed, Crease. After PSS today, I'll be there with you. Don't worry. Plenty of fools have threatened me with guns and they ended up gettin' whooped. I *got* you." He promised me. I had no choice but to trust him. He was all the backing I had. I didn't have one friend at Locke who would help me fight against Tariq Molten.

Mr. Richmond came charging up the aisle toward us. "Okay, Clapton. You've been doing better than usual, son. I'm sick of seeing your face in my office," he grumbled at Pacino.

"I'm sick of seeing your face . . . I mean . . . office, too, Mr. Richmond. You're looking at a brand-new Pacino Clapton. That's my word."

"Your word, huh?" Mr. Richmond gave Pacino a stare that didn't believe in the "new" Pacino's word. "All right. Don't let me down. You boys better get going." Mr. Richmond gave Pacino a pound, and then continued his march out of the auditorium.

"Yes, sir. I won't let you down, sir," Pacino called out. All I could do was nod, seeing how I've never had a real conversation with Principal Richmond. He and Pacino seemed like old golfing buddies from way back.

We grabbed our bags, and we headed off in separate directions. Pacino turned back toward me and said, "It'll be all right, Crease. That's my word."

I didn't say anything, just kept walking. Like Mr. Richmond, I wondered and hoped that Pacino's word was worth something. Anything at all.

2:48 P.M.
ALAIN LOCKE MIDDLE HIGH
THE PSS ROOM
THE LAST DAY

She looked like a lady today. Kinda nice.

"So what's all this for, girl? I know you're not trying to step up your game or something." Pacino kept sprinkling what sounded like hidden compliments to Rosilyn. I was worried out of my mind about what Tariq would or wouldn't try to do to me after school. But for a second, I took my mind off of that and noticed Rosilyn. She did look good.

Rosilyn rolled her eyes at Pacino. She smiled at both of us. "I don't know what you're talking about, fool. I always look good. Believe that."

She twisted around and showed off her beige-and-pink skirt. She had on a pretty silk blouse and some kind of gold necklace that she must have borrowed. Her hair was pinned up, and her hoop earrings clanked every time she worked her neck at Pacino. She even smelled different, something powdery and light. She still looked skinny to me, but her skirt and the rest of her outfit really caught my attention. No lie.

"I'm just saying you never dress up like this. The welfare or child custody people must be comin' by your house this evening, right?" Pacino is always trying to crack on that girl.

"You got jokes, huh? I know you like what you see." Rosilyn sucked her teeth. "Can't a girl just decide to look extra fly out of the blue? Quit hatin'."

"Please. Who said you looked fly? I didn't say that. Did you, Crease?" Pacino smirked at me, probably expecting me to front like he was doing.

"I didn't say it, but . . . you do look kinda sweet today, Rosilyn." I didn't know who looked more surprised, Pacino or Rosilyn.

"*Well*—I see somebody in here has got some taste. Forget you, Pacino." Rosilyn snapped her fingers like tiny firecrackers. Then she clacked her shiny brown heels back over to her workstation, put on her music, and zoned out.

Mr. Patt was on the phone. I thought he was talking to his wife because he kept saying "baby" and "honey." The filthy sixth grader Mackey didn't show up, which meant he had to make that day up and an extra one next week. Stupid sixth grader.

I don't know if Rosilyn had heard about Tariq having a gun. I turned my back on her and then leaned in closer to Pacino to ask him, "So . . . what are we gonna do?"

"Man, will you just chill. Dang! That punk got you all spooked. I shouldn't have told you."

My neck was heating up again, the fever spreading fast to my armpits. "So you are just going to let whatever is going to happen just happen?"

The only thing I kept imagining was a scene in a Bond movie with dozens of bullets flying at me. And no matter how fast I ran or how low I ducked, they would still tear through my clothes, pierce my skin, and slice my bones.

"How many times do I have to say I've got your back? He'll see me with you and turn around," Pacino bragged, like he was bulletproof. "I'm telling you, if I had your karate skills, I wouldn't be scared of anybody. Don't be an uppity momma's boy punk your whole life, Crease."

"*You're* the punk!" I yelled. Even Rosilyn heard me. She pulled one of her earbuds out and turned around.

Mr. Patt told his wife to hold on a second and then said to me, "Don't blow it or you'll be back here next week."

"I gotta be a punk or a momma's boy every time I don't say I want to knock somebody's teeth out? Or prove to you how hood I am? I'm sick of that." I was whispering, but I was heated.

"You don't need to be hood to protect yourself, fool."

"He may want to hurt me, but I won't play into that stupid stuff. I'm about using my mind, not fighting."

"Forget that!" Pacino said sharply. "Crease, those fools don't understand all of that mind and soul stuff you be poppin'. You need to tuck that in your karate bag—*brotha*."

Pacino would not give it up. He was preaching as much as Dad. "It would be cool if everybody called each other *brotha* or lived a fairy-tale life like you do, Crease, but we don't. Get over it," Pacino snapped. "If you're that scared, why don't you call one of your folks to come pick you up in one of their shiny cars?" Pacino pulled a cell phone out of his backpack and handed it to me.

"I don't want to worry them, especially if nothing's really gonna happen, right?"

I turned around to see if Rosilyn was paying attention. She wasn't. She was still listening to music, or at least I thought she was. She snatched her earbuds out, wrapped them around her phone, and then came back to Pacino's workstation.

"Look, Robeson, I can call my brothers up here. They don't like Tariq, either. I'm just sayin' if you need some help or something. I know fightin' ain't one of your things." Rosilyn looked at me so pitiful when she said that, like I was a wimp.

"I'm okay, Rosilyn. Thanks anyway. It's no big deal." I tried to be cool, but it wasn't working. Now all of me was hot.

Rosilyn gently ran her fingers across my cheek. "I just don't want them to mess up that cute face."

"Here we go. The lovebirds are at it again." Pacino cracked up.

"Leave Robeson alone. He can't help it if he thinks I'm fine," Rosilyn said.

"He can have your old—" Pacino started to say something foul, I could tell. But he stopped himself. "He can have you, Rosilyn. You can run off together, get married, and have a gang of rug rats. I don't care. But what he really needs to be concerned about now is what he's gonna do when that bell rings." Pacino stopped joking. He was all serious.

The bell never got a chance to ring.

Mr. Patt said his last "baby" and "honey," then got off of his cell phone, grinning like a fat man who had just won the pancake lottery. "Good news, delinquents. I know we usually dismiss at three thirty, but I've got something important to tend to, so I'm gonna let you go early. Out."

Pacino pumped a fist. Rosilyn waved her hands in the air. I gulped extra-extra hard.

I had a mad headache that was trying to pound itself out of my temples. The inside of my mouth was sandpaper. Sweat was coming fast to my face.

I would have done anything for more time in PSS.

2:59 P.M.
MEYER BOULEVARD
PARTING WAYS

Pacino didn't want to leave me hanging. He was standing by me, slow to leave. "I was gonna ride the Metro bus with you if you wanted me to. Your dad has a faculty meeting or something, right?"

"Yeah, he does. But I'll be okay," I told him, not sure if I'd be okay. In the back of my mind I could see Tariq and his boys patrolling every block around the school looking for me.

"I could go home, too. Moms is off from work today, plus she got paid so we might go to Red Lobster or something."

"Yeah, man. Go home. I'll be okay." I chuckled a little. I was tired of telling this nut to go home to be with his mom and sisters. I put my fist out to give Pacino a pound. Instead, he gave me half dap, half hug, like you do to one of your real boys. I guess that made us official—brothas. We stood in front of the rectangular fountain on Meyer, in the center of the boulevard. There wasn't a soul in sight. Not one car came or went. It was just Pacino and me, and a strange quiet for this time of day.

Pacino reached into his backpack. "Hey, man, I almost forgot. I still have your Dad's Miles Davis." He handed me the CD.

That's when I remembered. Today was Dad's Brand New Vision meeting.

"Wanna give him the CD yourself?"

Pacino hesitated. "You mean come back to your *Cosby Show* crib?"

"Yeah, to the Huxtable house," I joked.

"Nahhh, man, I got homework. And the twins are waiting on me, and my moms, too."

"There's some guys I want you to meet, friends of my dad's. It won't take long. You can be home in time for dinner."

"I'm not meeting any preachy dudes who like listening to classical tunes."

"Answer me this, Pacino. Did you like listening to Miles?"

Pacino was slow to admit it. "Miles is cool," he said.

"These brothers are all about cool," I said.

Pacino folded his arms tight. "I'm hungry. Do these all-about-cool brothers serve snacks?"

"Leftover lasagna."

"I can work with that." He hoisted his backpack, still holding on to the Miles CD. We walked to the bus stop, heading back to my house.

6:33 P.M.
BATTLEFIELD RESIDENCE
BRAND NEW VISION WEEKLY MEETING

Our family room was packed with members of an organization my dad started seven years ago, called Brand New Vision. These guys go to schools and walk the streets in the worst neighborhoods to mentor boys my age and older. Pacino and I busted in as the meeting was in full swing. We practically fell on top of each other.

"You brothas will have to excuse my son and his comrade," Dad apologized to his friends.

"Sorry, Dad. Sorry, guys."

Dad introduced Pacino to the group. "Fellas, I'd like you all to meet young Pacino Clapton." Greetings came from every point in the room, in scattered, deep voices.

Pacino waved. He looked a little scared, but curious, too. He never let go of his backpack. I'm sure he wasn't expecting to come into the middle of a room filled with some of the city's most successful, highly educated, and influential men.

Mom had left the lasagna, and the BNV members were enjoying it. Pacino and I helped ourselves to the lasagna and cleaned our plates before anyone else in the room. We were starvin' like a mug!

"Pacino is one of Alain Locke Middle's prized students. Am I correct?" Dad asked.

"Sure . . . I mean, yes, sir." Pacino set down his knapsack. The room was full of welcoming vibes.

A little wiry man with a gravelly voice and wide glasses, named Mr. Warren, was the first to speak to Pacino. He's the owner of a couple of bookstores in the city. He's also the father of six kids he's raising alone because his wife died. "Hey, little brotha. Keep doin' what you're doin'."

"Pacino, I would go around and introduce everyone, but that would take forever," Dad said. "If you and Robeson don't mind sitting in on the meeting, you could talk to some of the guys afterward. We don't have that much longer. We'd be honored if you stayed for the rest."

"That's cool, sir," Pacino said. He tried to sound all cool, but I could tell how excited he really was to join the group. He sat down before my dad even asked.

I raised my hand and agreed to stick around. "Me, too, Dad. I'll stay." We slid to the back of the room and sat at opposite ends of the fireplace. Pacino moved his bag out of the way so I could sit down. He seemed ready to listen, like folks are right before the preacher gets up to deliver a sermon.

My dad stood. "Okay, let's get back to it," he said to the group. He pointed at Mr. Merle, probably the tallest member of BNV. Mr. Merle used to play pro ball back in the eighties, before the Kings moved to Sacramento. Now he has the only black-owned golf course and country club in Missouri. He's married and has two kids.

"We were about to address the school district's decision to do away with the after-school programs. What are we going to do about that, Teddy?" Mr. Merle asked my dad.

"I say we go down there, all of us, and raise some hell," Mr. Sinclair said. "There are about three hundred of us between here and St. Louis. It just isn't right. What about those parents who work late and can't get off in time to pick up their kids?" Mr. Sinclair is married and runs the Boys and Girls Club over by Cleveland Avenue.

Soon the whole room got angry. The men were tossing around their ideas all at the same time, until my dad took control of the floor.

"All right, guys, quiet down, quiet down! We can't hear any of your ideas if everyone talks at once." The group got calm in a hurry. Dad set things off by throwing out a challenge: "Forget going down there ranting and raving. Let's start our own after-school program. We can do it. Who's with me?"

"What do you mean, Battlefield?" asked Deacon Luster, the oldest deacon at our church. He must be around eighty-seven, but still kickin'. He's a retired airline pilot, has been married for over fifty years, has five kids, and has more than twelve grandkids. "You mean you want us to go around to the schools and watch the kids?"

"That's exactly what I mean, deacon," Dad replied. "After all, as Sinclair has already pointed out, we're over three hundred strong."

Dad turned toward the rest of the group. "We have to stop depending on the school district, the government, and every other outside entity to look out for our children."

Pacino was watching, listening close, taking it all in. He paid special attention when Mr. Rayford, a young dude, spoke next.

"Sounds good, Mr. Battlefield, but how are we gonna reach *every* school?" Mr. Rayford works for that big J. E. Dunn Construction Company, and he's in school to be a civil engineer. He looked like a high school student to us. He was kinda slim with no facial hair at all.

"I'm glad you asked," Dad said. "There are enough of us to have at least two to three members at almost every building to organize after-school activities for the kids. We can make it happen."

That was my dad's favorite saying, and his motto for the Brand New Vision group—*We can make it happen.* Everything and anything is possible to my dad if enough energy is put behind it.

"Pacino? Did you want to add something?" Dad asked. Pacino had his hand raised, but not really. Dad called him out anyways.

Pacino cleared his throat. "I just don't get it. Why do *you* or anybody else in here care about where kids go after school? It's their momma's problem, right?" Everyone got quiet then. Pacino said, "I wouldn't spend my free time running all over to help someone else's kids. I got my own little sisters to watch after school."

The whole room turned around to lay eyes on Pacino. Then they all started to talk at once. Deacon Luster tapped his cane on the floor faster than I thought his old hands could move.

Somebody yelled out, "What did that boy say?"

Dad motioned for the group to quiet down. A few men threw their hands up, irritated.

Dad motioned for them to put their hands down. He said, "Pacino, you tell me. Why *should* we care?"

"That's what I'm saying. Folks have things to do, not to mention work. I know *I* have stuff to do." Pacino adjusted his jacket. "Babysitting a bunch of ungrateful kids ain't one of 'em."

"Robeson tells me you cut hair, right?" Dad asked.

"Yep. I can hook up the tightest fade you ever seen."

"Is that so?" Pacino nodded.

"Why do you do it?" Dad asked.

"Because I'm good at it, and I make a grip doin' it."

"Yeah, I know you get paid well, as smart as you are, but what do you do with the money?" Dad's gaze was all over Pacino, who sat still and answered everything thrown his way.

"I don't know. I buy clothes, kicks, video games. Stuff like that. But most of all, I help out my moms. Water bill, light bill, rent, whatever."

"You mean you give your mother money to pay bills and you look after your sisters? How much do you get for that? I bet you get paid, right?"

"Nope. They're my little sisters. If I don't do it, who else is gonna do it?" Pacino told Dad. He looked offended.

Another man, Mr. Wilkinson, who was new to BNV spoke next. "What he's saying is: does your mother have to make you stay at home and watch your little sisters? Did she *tell* you that you need to go out and make some extra money?" I didn't know Mr. Wilkinson as well as I did the other men. He was making a good point, though, and driving it home, too.

"No, she never had to ask me to do any of that stuff. It's just what I do," Pacino said. Dad walked toward Pacino.

"You don't have to do it, but your mother and your little sisters need you, and you should be proud of yourself. Are you?"

"Yeah, I guess. I never really looked at it that way."

"So what do you think would happen to your little sisters if you didn't watch after them, or if you didn't help your mother make ends meet with the bills?" Dad was right in front of Pacino now. He adjusted his glasses and folded his arms. Pacino leaned back against the fireplace.

"I guess they'd . . . I guess they'd have it bad," Pacino almost whispered as he looked to the floor.

"Hey, man, I know." Dad set his hand on Pacino's shoulder. "I grew up like you. I was the oldest. I had two little brothers, a little sister, and no dad. It was all me. I had to recognize my role, but it took me some time."

I was feeling for Pacino, too. He thought he'd only be getting leftovers and meeting some guys.

Pacino said, "Everybody here seems so important and so busy. When do you find the time to help anybody else?"

"You're not the only one with family members to look after. All of the men in here have positions ranging from janitors to judges. We've got fathers, grandfathers, husbands, single guys, you name it. But none of that matters. We *find* the time because we care about our community. Who's gonna do it if we don't?" Mr. Wilkinson added.

Pacino played with the zipper on his jacket.

Mr. Caruthers stood up, and asked my dad, "Hey, Teddy, did I hear the little brotha say he could cut the tightest fade you've ever seen?" Mr. Caruthers owns five barbershops and a chain of all-natural beauty supply stores. "Pacino, if you come to one of my shops, I'll let you check out some real artists, show you how it's done."

"Are you serious?" Pacino asked. "I bought all of my equipment from your supply shop on Troost."

"It's settled, then. I'll give you one of my cards and you ask your folks if it's okay," Caruthers said. It was the first time I had ever seen Pacino have that look of awe all over his face.

"Thanks, sir." Pacino shook Mr. Caruthers's hand and stuffed the card in his pocket. He had that look in his eyes. I had seen it a few times before when other boys have sat in on meetings. I could tell that being around all of these men changed the way he thought about a few things, if only for one night.

My dad stood before all of the BNV members and said, "Thank all of you brothas for coming. We'll discuss the next steps to take on the after school program in the upcoming days." Then he closed the meeting like he always does. "Let's move forward with power and purpose, men. May God continue to bless you all so that you may bless others. Good evening."

TROUBLE
ON
FRIDAY

3:13 P.M.
63RD AND INDIANA
THE SETUP

After school, I walked past Locke Senior High's football field, which runs adjacent to Indiana and the entire length of the 64th and 65th blocks. The football team was about to start practice.

No more PSS. This was the first evening this week where I'd be headed home straight after school. Dad had another faculty meeting at work, so he couldn't pick me up this evening either. I had to catch the Metro bus.

Halfway to 63rd street, I just remembered that I saw Pacino earlier in the day, and promised to meet him at the fountain on Meyer Boulevard at three-thirty. My dad wanted me to give him two more Miles Davis CDs to keep. Dad always says the three things we should never hesitate to give away are good books, good music, and good advice.

When I turned around to head back toward the fountain, I slammed face first into a wall. At least it felt that way. I was knocked smack dead on the sidewalk. When I looked up, it wasn't a wall at all—it was Poke and Chauncey, Tariq's boys.

"You just can't stay on your feet, can you? That's the second time this week that I've knocked you on your butt, boy," Poke, the lanky one, said.

Chauncey, the cocky kid, barked, "Get up, fool." He'd gotten his cornrows redone. They didn't look so ragged anymore. "Get up, dude," Chauncey repeated. "We ain't gonna do nothing."

"You looking crazy, man. You running from somebody?" Poke asked. He readjusted the shoulder pads and football helmet he was carrying on his back.

Chauncey dropped his football gear to his feet. Then he gripped one of my hands and yanked me up.

"Nah, I'm cool," I answered. "Where are you guys . . . I mean . . . what do you want?"

Poke said, "Man, we don't want anything from you. *You* ran into *us*."

I bit my lip. "I'm saying . . . the other day, the both of you and Tariq were going to . . . I didn't know what you were going to do." I braced myself and held up my clenched fists. "But I ain't no punk. Let's get it over with."

They paused, and then gawked down on me like I was a silly alien boy from the planet What's-His-Problem.

"Put your hands down, boy!" Chauncey slapped both of my fists toward the ground. "We don't have a problem with you."

Poke said, "Speak for yourself, Chauncey. I wanna slap the taste out of his funny-looking mouth!" Poke threw his football equipment down and pushed his lanky elbows and tight knuckles up to the sky. Then he started laughing. "Nah, I was just messin' with you man. You aiight."

Chauncey said, "Yeah, Battlefield. Soon as we found out who you was related to, that changed everything. For real."

"Who am I related to?"

Chauncey said, "Your pops. Mr. Battlefield. I owe him a lot."

"Me, too," added Poke. "If it wasn't for him, I don't know where we'd be. I'd probably have a room at that halfway house, group-home shack where Tariq lives."

"How do y'all know my dad?"

Chauncey ran down how he met Dad. "He rolled up on our block last year by himself. I think he was on his way around the corner from where we live to tutor some kids at the Genesis School. Something like that. I don't remember. We were about to scrap with somebody. I forgot who it was. Your pops jumped out of his car like he was the cops or something. Then he just broke us up."

Poke jumped in. "I remember that. First of all, he was lucky nobody jacked him for his ride, plus he was in the wrong hood to be playin' hero. Forty-fifth and South Benton? We thought he was crazy. But he did it anyway."

My dad is almost *crazy*-brave, but he'd never told me about stopping a fight on Forty-fifth and South Benton. "Yeah? What happened then?"

"Your dad started talkin' about why we shouldn't be fightin' and how he had just seen a police car around the corner," Chauncey said.

Poke jumped in again. "He said they'd take our black butts to jail just for being in the streets, and he knew that our parents didn't have money for bail. We cracked up at that 'cause he was right!"

"We respected him and squashed everything. It took a lot of guts to do what he did. Then he stuck around and started telling us about the history of our neighborhood and all of the black city leaders that were from our part of town." Chauncey looked over at Poke because he knew he was about to be interrupted again. But Poke let Chauncey continue.

"On top of all of that, he gave us some free passes to a basketball game at the Sprint Center and some flyers about his organization, called BNV. He said we could come by the new youth center on Cleaver Boulevard anytime in the evening. So we did."

Poke busted in. "And that's where we met Coach Thornton. We transferred from Central to Locke just to be on the JV football team."

Chauncey looked at me and said, "Hey, if your pops is that cool, we figured his son can't be that bad. Plus, Tariq is crazy. We've known him since he was in the first grade. I thought he just wanted to punk you in the stairs the other day. Not really do anything, just scare you. I've kinda chilled out on all that fighting for no stupid reason. I wasn't gonna get in trouble for that fool."

Turned out these guys were cool. I wasn't so scared of them now.

"Yeah, it was stupid," I told them. But I still had an eye out for Tariq. "Where is he now? Did you hear that he had a gun today?"

Poke cut a look to Chauncey. "Oh yeah. He did. I saw it myself. But I'm done with that chump. Tariq ain't nothing but trouble. I mean, I ain't got no problem roughing up somebody up if they deserve it, but Tariq just don't care."

Chauncey picked up his football gear off of the sidewalk. "But on the real, you don't have to worry about Tariq messin' with you. He's after some other dude, like *for real, for real* after this dude."

I didn't even ask why Tariq wasn't after me anymore. Poke and Chauncey were about to cross the street and cut through a gap in a chain-link fence. They were running late to practice. I asked, "Why is he after that other dude?"

"They just don't get along, so Tariq said he's gonna take care of it. That's all I know," Poke said before he eyed a slit in the fence across the street for him to slide his skinny frame through.

"C'mon, man, tell me who's on Tariq's 'hit' list?" I asked.

"As long as it ain't you, just stay away from Tariq," Chauncey answered.

But it was Poke who gave it up. "The kid's name is *P*-something. Pacheeko, or Paccino. Something crazy like that."

Chauncey bumped me. "We gotta go, Battlefield. Get off of these streets, boy." The two of them took off toward practice.

That's when the wrecking ball hit me. Everything stopped. My brain shut down immediately. My body took over. I just started running. I ran like a genetically engineered track star. The 64th and 65th blocks of Indiana became a blur of bushes and mail boxes.

The front lawn of the senior building is the length of a football field. I don't think my feet touched the ground though. I cleared it in seconds. What would I do when I got there? Would I be too late?

The fountain.

When I got to the fountain, Pacino was there—and so was Tariq.

3:22 P.M.
MEYER BOULEVARD
THE FOUNTAIN

Tariq was at the edge of the fountain, holding a small gun to Pacino's chest. They looked like statues. Neither one of them spoke or moved. Their reflections danced back and forth in the water.

Tariq turned around and saw me. I'd startled him. "Look who's here. You just can't stay away from trouble, can you?" The arm that he held the gun up with started to shake a little bit. He looked back at Pacino, then smiled at me like he had just landed a two-for-one deal. "You must be the most unluckiest fool ever."

Pacino looked at me but didn't say a word. He blinked, licked his lips. He was wearing his gray-and-blue Royals cap, cocked to the back. His arms were at his sides, his bag at his feet. He looked calmer than Tariq did.

"I was just . . . I was just . . . on my way home and . . ." I stuttered.

Tariq spoke slowly, carefully. "You don't live over here. You're too white-bread to live on this side of the fountain."

"I was meeting—"

"Unless you wanna see this dude get lit up, you need to keep movin'." Tariq pressed the gun deeper into Pacino's chest.

"I can't do that. Why don't you just . . . put the gun away, man?"

"I ain't saying it no more. Leave!" He grabbed Pacino by the collar, then pointed the gun at me with the other hand. I dropped my bag.

"Go 'head, man. Leave like he said, Crease!" Pacino was wincing, pleading.

Tariq looked back and forth between us. "Crease, is this your girlfriend or something?" Tariq was crazy with that gun, shaking it and looking scared and wild, too. "I got enough slugs in here for the both of you."

I lowered my head, dropped my hands to my side, and closed my eyes. If I was going to get shot, I didn't want to see it.

"What are you doing, praying?" he asked. "I don't know why you wasting your time praying. You're about to talk to God face-to-face in a minute." This was a joke to Tariq, a game.

Finally, Pacino spoke. "He ain't done nothing to you, you little punk. Leave him alone."

My eyes were still closed. I tried to take my mind to another place. I was almost wishing something would happen to get this over with.

When I opened my eyes, Pacino was swinging at Tariq. Tariq jerked back, avoiding the punch, but he still had a tight grip around Pacino's neck. "What was that, huh?" He swung the gun like a sling blade and opened up the right side of Pacino's face. Blood rushed down Pacino's cheek, onto his clothes and the ground.

His head slumped, but somehow he was still on his feet. Tariq took one look at me and said, "This one is for you." Then he reached all the way back, like he was swinging a pick axe, and came down with the butt of the gun smack dead between Pacino's eyes. It was like lightning struck his forehead. His cap flew off of his head, and spun like a helicopter seed into the fountain. The blow was enough to drop him to his knees, and finally flat to the pavement.

Tariq turned to me then. "You know—I never did like you," he said.

Disarming somebody with a weapon was one of the first things I learned when I started studying kyokushin. It would've been easy to do with Tariq, but he was too far away from me and he was about to go off on some messed-up rampage.

He started laughing all loud. "Look at you baby fools." He couldn't stop cracking up. "You look like you're about to pee in your diapers. I don't need bullets to lay you out. You just two soft, sissy-made punks."

Right then, Tariq pulled the pistol's trigger three times fast—*click, click, click*. I *did* nearly wet my pants but saw right off that the gun wasn't loaded.

I looked over, and was surprised to see Pacino slowly rising to his feet—wet, still spitting blood, and wiping his face. He just wouldn't stay down.

Tariq came running at me with the gun over his head. Pacino lunged in to help me. "Crease!" he shouted, grabbing Tariq. The gun flew from Tariq's hand. He stopped, his eyes got wide. He knew he was about to get it.

Tariq swung out a weak punch, first at Pacino, then at me. I blocked it, and then gave him a knife-hand to the neck. He was bent over, gagging, gasping, finding his balance. That's when I grabbed the back of his head with both hands and came up with a strong knee kick, first to his nose, then to his mouth and to his head. He fell backward and smacked hard to the pavement.

I kept kicking until I felt Tariq's warm blood on my pants leg.

When I finally let up, my knee was numb and tingling. Tariq staggered onto his feet, blowing blood and spit. He tried to come at me but couldn't. He was confused, like a drunk who couldn't make sense of stuff that was happening too fast. He tripped backward and stayed down, still struggling and half conscious.

My heart felt like it was a hundred pounds. Pacino grabbed the gun, and then came to me. He was still bleeding from his head and face. "You all right, Crease?" I didn't answer. I *couldn't* answer. I couldn't stop crying.

I was no different from Tariq for what I had done to him. Yeah, Tariq hadn't given me much of a choice, but I'd slammed everything I stood for. I tried to bite down on the crying, but it was holding on. I wanted to give Tariq another kick, but he was down for good, though. I walked Pacino slowly to the edge of the fountain. We sat down and I put an arm around his shoulder. "Thanks, brother," was all he said.

Cars began to circle the fountain. Then people started showing up, running to help.

A lady with two Labradors took off her jacket and covered Tariq with it. A girl hopped off her bike and offered her coat to Pacino. The lady with the dogs asked me, "Baby, are you okay? How did all of this happen?" I wiped my nose with my sleeve, still not ready to speak.

5:48 P.M.
RESEARCH MEDICAL CENTER
WAITING

"Robeson, look at me when I talk to you."

But I couldn't lift my eyes to meet Dad's, not even for a second.

It was Mr. Wilkinson, Dad's friend from BNV, who got me to look up. I knew he was a policeman, but I'd never seen him in uniform. "Tariq's hurt badly, and we need your help."

The hospital hallway was busy with other policemen, nurses, families, announcements flying in and out of a loudspeaker, and us.

Pacino had been taken to another room. When we got to the hospital in a police car, they refused to keep us together, even though we'd told the police that we *were* together—that it wasn't us fighting against each other.

Tariq had been put into an ambulance at the fountain, and I had no idea what had happened to him after that.

Mr. Wilkinson lifted my chin. He wouldn't let me escape his gaze.

"Robeson, I'm what they call a youth aid investigator. I'll be handling things along with another investigator that's been in the Juvenile Investigation Unit for over twenty years. He's worked with the parole officer of that Tariq Molten kid many times."

Dad was inspecting my shirt, which was covered with blood specks. He hugged me.

"Does Mom know?" I asked.

"She's flying back from Maryland now."

I asked Mr. Wilkinson, "How are Pacino and Tariq doing?"

"Pacino's fine. He's given us some of the details we need. They're going to keep him overnight for observation, but he's in good shape." I wasn't expecting the news on Tariq to be good, though. Usually, people give the worse of two pieces of news last. I was right.

"Tariq's situation is a little bit trickier. He's fading in and out of consciousness." Mr. Wilkinson was relaying to us what the doctors had told him. There was worry in his voice. "Tariq's nose is broken, and he's suffered a grade-three concussion."

"Will he be okay?"

"The doctors said that he'll more than likely suffer some serious memory loss when he wakes up," Mr. Wilkinson said.

I was so scared, I let out a breath.

Mr. Wilkinson said, "The paramedics got there just in time. A couple more minutes and Tariq wouldn't have made it." Mr. Wilkinson shook his head. "The good Lord was with you fellas today, Robeson."

"I've been praying all afternoon," Dad said.

Mr. Wilkinson jumped in. "That's another thing, Robeson. We found the gun by the fountain. It was stolen and it had Tariq's prints all over it. And there was a witness who saw him holding it on you and your friend."

Dad said, "I don't even want to imagine what would have happened if the gun was loaded." I was ready for Dad to tell me I was no longer a Battlefield, that I didn't deserve to keep our family name. And I knew a lecture was coming. But Dad was more concerned with me, Tariq, and Pacino. "Sometimes in life, Robeson, you do what a situation calls for. You may surprise yourself, and react in a way that you never knew you were capable of. I'm just glad you're safe." Dad hugged me again.

"Your father is right, Robeson. Your friend Pacino is on the third floor with his family, waiting to tell you thanks." Mr. Wilkinson jabbed me in the arm, like Pacino does.

"What about Tariq?" I asked.

"The boy's got no family to speak of. We called his grandparents, but no one answered. We even called the group home where he lives, but nobody's shown up yet. He's by himself."

6:07 P.M.
RESEARCH MEDICAL CENTER, ROOM 7647
PACINO'S ROOM

Mr. Wilkinson showed me and Dad to where Pacino was on the third floor. Pacino's mom welcomed us as soon as we arrived in the room where they were keeping an eye on Pacino overnight. He had a huge knot on his forehead and the right side of his face was bandaged. Other than that, he looked fine.

"You must be Crease. Come on in, baby. I'm Mrs. Clapton, Pacino's momma, but everybody calls me Missy." She hugged Dad and me like we were family. Dad hugged her back, just like he does to his sister, my aunt Vanessa, when it looks like she really needs a nice strong hug. "I've heard so much about you both, good stuff, too. Find a seat somewhere."

For a woman who works two jobs, she greeted us with a wave of energy. She looked anything but tired. She had long lashes like a movie star, and her almond eyes were a shade of brown that I had never seen. But her wide and welcoming smile was something that I see every single day of my life—it was my mother's.

The Clapton family was deep in the hospital room. There were at least fifteen people crammed in. There were already flowers and get-well cards in the room.

Pacino's twin sisters and four other kids were watching *Steven Universe* on the TV hanging in the corner of the room.

Ms. Clapton and I were able to ease through the crowded room of family members to stand next to Pacino's bed. Dad found it harder to squeeze through. He just stood at the door and held a conversation with one of the men in the room. I think he was an uncle or cousin. I recognized him from the wall of pictures at Pacino's apartment.

"Look, I just want to tell you thanks, Crease. Really, baby," Ms. Clapton said.

"No problem, Ms. Clapton. He would have done the same thing for me."

Pacino was sitting up in the bed. He was glad to see me and Dad. As I leaned in closer, I noticed that his right eye was swollen. Dried blood spots were seeping through his bandages.

I leaned close and spoke quickly. "Pacino. It's me. It's Crease, man."

"Man, what are you whispering for? I ain't dying, fool." Pacino moaned, but he was smiling, too. He held a hand up and I grabbed it, squeezed it tight. He was going to be okay. I felt it in his grip.

"Same old Pacino. Boy, you better be glad I showed up to save your sorry butt," I joked with him.

"Saved me? Somebody told you wrong, Crease. Nobody needs to save me. Ya dig?" He closed his eyes and winced.

"Just lay back, man." I helped him recline a little.

Pacino's mother handed him a cup of ice water. "Man, can you tell my moms that men like us need *food*. I'm hungry! They got some fries to go with that water? I got the taste for a beef on bun barbeque sandwich, too."

"And some slaw," I added.

"And some baked beans. Crease, hand me my jacket and shoes. We getting out of here."

We both cracked up. Pacino looked tired.

"Hey, man, rest," I said. "Tomorrow evening, my dad and I can bring you some grub."

"I'm getting out of here in the morning. I'm cool, Crease. I guess I can live on hospital food for one night."

Dad left the room to answer a call. Pacino's mother was busy with the twins.

Pacino asked, "So where is your boy Tariq? I bet the cops got him all hemmed up."

"No, man, he's right here in this hospital."

Pacino said, "Tell the nurse to give my hospital food to *him*." We both laughed.

"I got your back," I said. "You've had mine all week, so I owe you."

Pacino said, "Man, you've been tough enough today. Save your fight for the streets." I gave Pacino a pound, and we laughed together again. I didn't care anymore if he thought I was tough enough or hard enough or cool enough. All I knew was that when it mattered most, I was *friend enough.*

"You need anything? Looks like more people are coming in. I better go." I asked Pacino.

"I'm cool. I'm cool. Go 'head, man. Tell your dad that I was wearing a belt when all of this stuff went down. At least I looked presentable when I got bashed in the face, right?" he laughed at his own joke.

I chuckled a little, and said, "You can keep the belt."

"Thanks. I owe you, huh?" he said before he took a bite out of the hospital hamburger on his tray, and then spit it right back out.

I thought about everything that happened earlier and said, "Nah, you don't owe me anything, Pacino. Just get better. That's all."

He didn't owe me a thing. We were boys.

SOLUTIONS
ON
SATURDAY

6:14 P.M.
RESEARCH MEDICAL CENTER

Dad and I went back to the hospital the next day to visit Pacino and to check out the situation with Tariq.

Pacino was in his room with his mom, packing to go home. He looked good. He and the twins were playing cards and laughing.

"I brought you some of my mom's mousse cake."

"Thanks, man." Pacino was definitely feeling better. He sliced off some of the cake to share with the twins, and ate the rest quickly.

"Hey, I'm outta here," he said. "See you at Locke on Monday," Pacino said.

"But not in PSS."

Pacino bumped me. "You know it."

6:29 P.M.
RESEARCH MEDICAL CENTER
ROOM 7654–TARIQ'S ROOM

"I'm talking serious, *serious* trouble. We don't have any tolerance for menaces to society like this kid!"

I heard an unfamiliar voice coming from Tariq's hospital room. That voice made me think of Pacino accusing me of "talking white," which was stupid. I peeped through the little glass rectangle in the door and was surprised to see that it was a Black dude. The brotha sounded like one of those Republican negroes that my dad can't stand.

"What are we looking at? Aggravated assault? Gun possession? It was a stolen gun at that. This poor little brotha's rap sheet is going to be a mile long by the time he's twenty." I heard Mr. Wilkinson say. I stood out in the hallway. I didn't want to just bust in.

"What poor little brother? He's a criminal. A miscreant." The old dude grumbled.

Dad saw me standing out in the hallway and yelled out, "Robeson, son, come on in. I want you to meet someone."

"Oh . . . okay, Dad." I walked in and Mr. Wilkinson and the old uppity dude turned to me. Mr. Wilkinson smiled, but the other man sneered at me like I was

Tariq. His sharp, trimmed, silver goatee and ice cold stare didn't make me feel welcome. He had on a pair of expensive looking glasses, and a spotless, grey, pin-striped suit. His shoes looked like they were just polished down in the lobby. There was a gold badge clipped to his alligator belt.

"How's it going, young man," the officer stuck out his hand to me. I was for sure he wanted the regular handshake—no pound, nothing fancy. "I'm Officer Watts. We're going to make sure that this boy gets everything he deserves for attacking you and your friend. More than likely, he'll just end up at the Boonville Correctional Facility. They all do. I'm sure this one is no different."

I looked over at Tariq in his bed and he didn't move one inch. He almost looked dead. That didn't stop Officer Watts from talking about him like he was a ghost in the room. That caught me way off guard.

"Well, sir, I just left my friend's room to see how he was doing. I think he's going to be fine," I told Officer Watts. He walked over to the only window in the room to nab his briefcase off of a table.

The blinds were closed. There were no teddy bears holding balloons, no flowers, and there was no TV high in the corner entertaining visitors. The room was vacant of the laughter in Pacino's room. There was only silence, a lonely silence. There were no visitors, family, or friends of the family to see about the well being of Tariq.

"So you said Pacino was fine, huh, son?" Dad asked.

"Oh yeah. He's fine, Dad."

"That's good. Real good." And that's all he said. He folded his arms, stood next to Mr. Wilkinson, and stared off, deep in thought. I couldn't believe that he didn't have any input. He looked like his thoughts were not that clear yet. But I could tell that he wasn't too fond of Officer Watts though. I knew that.

"Alright, here we are," Officer Watts came back and joined the semicircle of me, Dad, and Mr. Wilkinson at the foot of Tariq's bed. He had a thin stack of official looking papers in his hand. "Here's a background on the boy. I've been doing this for some time, right Wilkinson, and young punks like this are never going to amount to squat. What a shame." He snipped and snorted a self-righteous laugh.

"So what has he done within the past twenty-four months? Anything serious?" Mr. Wilkinson wanted to know all of the facts before he went forward with anything.

"Let's see here," Officer Watts thumbed through the records. "It looks like eight months ago he was an accessory in the robbery of a taxi cab with two other thieves.

"Anything else?" Dad asked.

"Almost four months ago it seems he was picked up on another assault charge. Before that, he had a couple of petty thefts, vandalism—same old story. But these are enough misdemeanors for me to do what needs to be done," he expressed to my dad.

"So what was the assault about, the last one?" Mr. Wilkinson asked. He looked like he was taking notes in his head. My dad just stood there quiet.

"It says something about a burglary at his grandmother's house. Allegedly, he found out who it was, or who he *thought* it was, and viciously attacked two other boys with a baseball bat. Typical, dumb street behavior. These boys will never learn. Jail seems like the only solution." Officer Watts gave us that obnoxious laugh again.

I could see the anger swelling up in Dad. I just knew that at any moment my dad was going to go off on that man. But he just chilled.

"Well, what about juvenile court or some sort of diversion program? His offenses aren't that bad. We've seen worse, at least since I've been in the unit." Mr. Wilkinson sounded like he wanted to give Tariq a break. Officer Watts made it clear that he had no connection to the boy lying in the bed with tubes and beeping machines attached to his body. That's the vibe I was getting.

I couldn't believe that my dad just stood there and looked confused. All he said was, "If that's what has to be done, that's what has to be done."

"Believe me, you don't want this boy back out on the streets," Officer Watts said as he slid on and buttoned up his heavy, charcoal Brooks Brothers' overcoat.

"Come on now, Watts. You don't believe this young man can change?" Dad responded.

"Well, Dr. Battlefield, this 'young man' as you so loosely tossed out, could've killed your boy and another one."

"There has to be something we could do with him when he wakes up instead of sending him straight to prison. His mother is missing in action, and we have no record of his father." Mr. Wilkinson made one last effort to take it easy on Tariq.

By this time, I didn't know how to feel. I knew that there was no way Tariq was going to get a slap on the wrist, and he didn't deserve one. I just thought that maybe Officer Watts could have done something. But all he wanted was to throw Tariq in jail like he's probably done to hundreds of other boys, Black boys like Tariq, like Pacino . . . like me.

"You fellas stand around and think of something to do with him and I'll head on out." He turned to make his way to the door, and tipped his brim like he was a gentleman.

I've been to enough Brand New Vision meetings and actually seen my dad solve tough situations before. If he wasn't going to make a move, for whatever reason, I had to.

I thought it would probably sound strange coming from me, but I said something on Tariq's behalf anyway. "Wait a minute, sir. I have an idea. There is something that can be done."

Officer Watts rolled his eyes. Mr. Wilkinson took a seat and anxiously waited for whatever was going to come out of my mouth. The look on my dad's face was like nothing I'd ever seen before. It was shock, it was surprise; it was almost like pride but more like amazement.

"Don't tell me that *you*, of all people in this room, want to see what's best for this kid?" Officer Watts looked so disappointed, but I was too; at him as a Black man and a little bit at my Dad for not stepping up.

"What kind of idea do you have, Robeson? Why the change of heart?" It was the first hint of confusion I'd ever heard in my Dad's voice, ever.

"It's not really a change of heart; I never really had anything against Tariq. Plus, I know that there is something that you guys can do, right, Dad?" I stood before them like I was Tariq's guardian angel. "Stuff like this is what you made the group for. You formed it for boys like Tariq. He needs help bad. Look at him. He's somebody like us. He deserves another chance, doesn't he?"

"No. No he doesn't," Officer Watts interrupted. "If his parents were around to teach him how to be a moral citizen, like I'm sure your parents are, he wouldn't be lying in that bed. Everyone only has one shot, kid. That's it." Officer Watts wasn't budging.

Mr. Wilkinson looked like he was deep in thought. Then he pulled out his iPhone and started scrolling through it.

"Officer Watts, don't be so stupid! If my dad or everybody else thought like you . . . we'd be up a creek without a paddle or the boat." I just snapped. "If Tariq had a dad like mine, or a mother like mine, maybe he wouldn't be in so much trouble all the time. But he doesn't have all of that stuff."

"Son, watch your mouth!" Dad jumped at me. "Officer Watts may not be on the level, but he's still an adult."

"It's okay, Dr. Battlefield. I see what kind of disrespect you are instilling in your boy. He's just lucky that gun didn't have any bullets in it."

"And what do you mean by that?" Dad clinched his fists, took a deep breath and then laid into Officer Watts. "My son can't say it, but I can. You are a disgrace to human beings everywhere. You're the real piece of trash, Watts!" Dad was fuming.

"Calm down everyone! Let's at least hear what Robeson is suggesting," said Mr. Wilkinson. Everyone stopped jabbering and turned to me.

"Well, Dad, there has to be one of the Brand New Vision members that can take some type of custody of Tariq. Do you know somebody that might want to take a chance on him? Maybe *we* can do something. Who's going to look after him?" I was saying the things I was expecting my dad to say.

"Son, I feel where you're coming from. I do. I've been thinking the same thing ever since we've been in this room. But the only thing that has stopped me is . . . is you," Dad explained. "I've helped all kind of kids, just like Tariq. But I've never reached out to one that could have killed one of my very own kids. I guess I was just torn, son. That's all."

I put my hand on his shoulder, just like he's done to me a million times, and told him, "Don't be torn, Dad. Do what you do best—help people. You help people who are in a bad way. You tell me all the time about how the jails are filled with *us*. Well here's one we can keep out. Tariq's no different, is he?"

"Nope. He isn't, son. If we don't help him, who will?" Dad remarked. He burned a hole through Officer Watts' face like he had laser beams for eyes.

"So what is it that you guys suggest, Battlefield? Wilkinson?" Officer Watts dropped his briefcase, sighed like he had just lost an intense battle, and folded his arms in disgust.

Mr. Wilkinson stopped flipping through his iPhone, looked up at us, and grinned like he had just found the answer to a hidden mystery. "Got it! Theodore, you remember Yancey Bettis? He used to play football for MU and the Bengals about twelve or thirteen years ago."

"Yeah, kinda. I didn't get a chance to talk to him. He came with you and a couple of other new members last month, right?" my dad responded.

"Right. Well his brother-in-law was telling me last week that he and Yancey have a 140-acre ranch in Nicodemus, Kansas for troubled young brothas: homeless, abused, in trouble with the law, bad luck, whatever. It's been operating for almost a year now."

"I knew you fellas had something up your sleeves!" I hollered. It felt like everything was falling in place.

The best part was seeing the look on Officer Watts' face. It looked like he had an upset stomach. "You all are crazy." My dad and Mr. Wilkinson ignored him though. They just kept right on planning the next steps for Tariq like he was one of their sons.

"How'd Bettis get all of that organized? Government funds? Rich parents?" Dad asked.

"I guess it was from his playing days. It's all his money, bruh. They all don't just blow everything on cars and jewelry. He said he'd always been interested in creating a home for wayward kids. By the time Tariq is released from here, he'll be ready for the ranch. I think the name of it is The Hope of Onyx. Don't you think this is perfect for him?" Mr. Wilkinson asked Dad.

"All you have to do now is get in contact with Bettis and we can get this settled." Dad said with that confidence I'm used to hearing. That was the dad I knew.

"I'll step outside and give him a call right now. I'll handle this case myself, Theodore. You can count on me. Back in a minute." Mr. Wilkinson just blew by Officer Watts and jetted out the door.

Officer Watts shook his head at Dad and said, "You just don't know what you're getting into. I've seen your kind, the do-gooders. Always thinking you can save the world. You can't."

"Watts—you really need to retire and go into something that really suits your personality and passions. You've done enough damage to our community. We'll take it from here, *sir*." Dad opened the door to let Officer Watts out.

He tipped his brim again and said, "You're gonna be sorry, Battlefield. They never change. You'll see." Dad slammed the door without even answering. He'd had enough of Officer Watts.

"I'm going out here with Mike to see what I can do to help out. You gonna be okay?" Dad asked me.

I looked over at Tariq, and from where I stood, he was still dead to the world. I know they said he'd be alright, but it felt like the beeping machines and tubes were the only things keeping him alive. "Yeah, Dad, I'm cool. Go 'head."

Before he left the room, he gave me a hug and held it for a few seconds. It wasn't a half pound-half hug. It was a real type of hug; the type that fathers give to their sons; and the type that men give to someone that they really respect.

He looked at me and whispered, "Thank you, son." I didn't say anything. I just hugged him back. He turned and left out of the room again but slower, his shoulders broad, his head high; he turned on that strong Battlefield swagger I hoped to perfect someday. I was in the room with Tariq, alone.

The last time I stood over Tariq, I felt ashamed about what I had done, and I was worried about his life. When I stood at the foot of his hospital bed, by myself, I didn't feel so ashamed anymore. I felt relieved. I wasn't so worried about his life. I felt hopeful.

I walked over to his bedside and the first thing I noticed was his chest heaving. He looked like he was breathing normal. Then I noticed some type of oxygen mask strapped to his mouth. His nose was fitted and wrapped with a heavy looking brace.

I leaned in a little closer and hung my head over the side of his bed like people do to coffins at funerals. His face was still swollen but had turned purple all over. I saw anger in his cheeks and his eyes began to twitch and water. And just for a second, maybe even less, I could have sworn he opened his eyes and looked straight at me.

"I know you're sick of me, man," I mumbled to him. Obviously he didn't respond, but I just kept talking. "Look, I know we can't turn back time or anything, so uh . . . we're just gonna have to move on from this. I never meant to hurt you. That's the honest-to-God truth. And somehow, I know deep inside of there, that you don't really like hurting people either." I pulled up a chair and sat next to the bed. I became his only visitor.

"When you wake up from this, you might hate me forever. But you know, maybe this ranch thing would be better than what that cop had planned for you. Really . . . you owe me. I stood up for you, man. You owe me." I chuckled to myself.

The nurse that was in Pacino's room tipped her head in the door and said, "Making your rounds, huh?"

"I'll get out of your way soon." I replied.

"No, it's okay. I'll come back. These boys have a real good friend in you."

She had no idea how right and wrong she was.

The door to the room closed slowly, and I kept right on talking to Tariq. "I know we haven't had the best history and everything—but I'm pulling for you. I am."

I scooted my chair as close as I could get it to his bedside. I rested my elbows on my knees, put my hands together, closed my eyes and prayed. I don't even remember everything I said, but it was good. It was full of every good thing I wished I could see in Tariq's life.

When I raised my head and opened my eyes, he was still asleep. The machines still beeped. The tubes were all in place. But that empty, lonely feeling in the room wasn't as heavy as it was before. While I was there, no one ever showed up that evening. But I stayed there by his side for as long as I could.

He never gave a sign that he could hear my prayer, and that was okay by me. I had hoped that when Tariq Molten woke up, and I was long gone, that God would tell him everything that I said.

Every single word.

BROTHERS

10:25 A.M.
ARROWHEAD STADIUM

"Now aren't you glad we stopped and picked up that hat and scarf, boy? You were gonna freeze your butt off if we didn't." Dad jabbed at Pacino from the driver's seat. We pulled into the jammed packed parking lot of Arrowhead Stadium behind a train of other cars filled with Chiefs fans.

"I would've came here shirtless with paint all over my body like one those crazy White boys." Pacino answered. It was three months after the whole fountain incident. His headaches were gone. The stitches were out. To tell the truth, we barely talked about it.

"Yeah, and you would've caught pneumonia like one of those 'crazy White boys.'" I told him. We picked up Pacino and headed straight to Gates and Sons. I promised him a beef on bun sandwich and that's what I did. We went there and killed a whole platter of ribs, sandwiches, baked beans, and fries. We always stop there before a big game.

"I don't mind getting sick if my team can pull off a big win against the Chargers today. We'll win the division, get home-field advantage, sweep everybody, and finish out December at thirteen and two. *I'll take a nice hot case of pneumonia, please.*" Pacino held a finger up and ordered like he was at a restaurant. Carmichael was sitting in the back seat with me. He cracked up at Pacino as he looked out his window.

"Pacino, you're something else, son," Dad laughed too. We were about six cars back from the pay booth. He looked ahead at the price posted up and said, "Forty dollars? Robbery is what it is. But I guess as long as they're winning, these diehard fans will pay it." Dad always complains about the high price even though parking passes come with his season tickets package.

"So the whole gang is out here, huh, Daddy?" Carmichael asked.

"We bought up to one hundred and twenty tickets for this game. Every member is bringing a guest or guests."

"Like me. I'm the Battlefield guest, right, Doc?" Pacino said to Dad.

"Yeah right, you're a *guest*. You come over so much now, it's like you're one of these big headed boys." Dad jabbed at Pacino again.

"This is my first time being at a NFL stadium. I appreciate this. I do." Pacino said seriously at the tail end of a laugh. "I'm just surprised that Crease picked me over . . . Rosilyn. What did you do? Tell her you were going out of town or something? Love is a beautiful thang, right fellas?" Pacino loved to put me on the spot whenever it came to Rosilyn.

"Yeah, so what. She's my new girl. You're just jealous, fool." Dad and Carmichael started making kissing sounds. I didn't care.

"I'm just saying. She's a hood chick, Crease. You might be getting in over your head," Pacino kept picking at me. "You know she's gonna have ya nose wide open? You know that right?"

"She might be from the hood, but that don't make her a hood chick. She's a queen . . . my queen. Any of you got a problem with that?" I responded, serious as a mug. He wasn't going to make me feel embarrassed.

"Okay, okay, let's get off of Robeson. We're out here for the game, men," Dad said, still laughing. "Tailgating at Arrowhead is a rite of passage, Pacino.

You'll see." He was just as excited as we were about the game.

Dad was right though. Arrowhead is the only place I've ever seen in the city where people from all different backgrounds pull together for one purpose—a win!

The wind whips around the stadium, and the temperature dips around twenty below, but no one minds. The snack vendors walk up and down the steps throwing hotdogs and pouring cup after cup of hot chocolate from special hot chocolate back packs. And at the end of the National anthem, the part that says . . . *O'er the land of the free*, eighty-thousand Chiefs fans thunder out . . . *home of the CHIEFS!!!* My ears vibrate and ring. Every bone in my body rattles. It makes you want to almost jump out on the field and tackle somebody yourself.

Carmichael and I have been lucky enough to experience that dozens of times. Now, Pacino was with us. I was just happy for him. I was just happy to be together, all four of us.

"I got it, Daddy," Carmichael said. Dad pulled up to the pay booth, and rolled down the back window on Carmichael's side. "Here you go, brotha," my little brother said, as he passed the man the parking passes.

Dad parked in section J-58, right across from the big Brand New Vision tailgating tent. Before we even opened the car doors we could smell the big stacks of barbeque smoke.

"Hey guys, the game doesn't start for another hour, and I know we just left Gates, but if you still got room for more, were gonna head on over to the tent," Dad announced. He dug into his wallet and pulled out five twenties. He turned to all three of us and dealt the money out like playing cards. "Here's forty a piece for the two big brothers and twenty for the little one. That should be enough, right?"

"Right!" Pacino, Carmichael and I answered. Even though I knew that Pacino probably already had a fat roll of haircut-hustle money in his pocket.

"Let's get out, daddy. I see Marco and Raheem!" Carmichael spotted two of his buddies.

"Okay, son. Come with me," Dad put on his hat and gloves and got out of the car with Carmichael. Then he leaned his head back inside and said, "Pacino, Robeson, you two get the stuff out of the back and then meet us across the street in the tent. And don't forget to lock the doors." He grabbed his scarf and then tossed me the keys.

"We got it, Dad," I answered.

"Yeah, *Dad*, we got this." Pacino added. Dad just grinned at us both and shut his door.

Pacino and I got out and were about to open the hatchback and grab the blankets, extra hoodies, and the little heat packs that you put in your shoes. But we had a change of plans when we saw six of the Chiefs cheerleaders going into the tent. Four of them were Black, which is rare because they almost never have Black cheerleaders.

"Did you see that? Forget these blankets. Let's go over to the tent!" Pacino almost jumped out of his winter gear. "Let's go get a picture, a phone number or something."

"I'm with you. The game doesn't start for another hour, right?"

"Right." Pacino nodded, looked both ways, and jetted across the street.

I followed just as fast. The cold wind whistled by my ears and paralyzed my face for a second.

"Hurry up, man!" Pacino yelled out.

But as soon as I made it to the other side of the street, I remembered, "Dang! I forgot to lock the doors."

"Yeah, you go back and do that while I go inside and make some new cheerleading friends." Pacino turned his back on me and then tip-toed in the tent like a sneaky fox.

Vans and school buses, painted red and gold with Chiefs logos, kept me from going back across the street. Then there were a couple of Metro buses that rolled by. In between each vehicle, I could see people in the parking lot waiting on their turns to cross.

When the traffic slowed, there was one gigantic dude trekking across the crosswalk by himself. He looked like he could've been a Chief, probably an offensive tackle or defensive end. His shoulders were as wide as the length of my whole body. There were a bunch of boys behind him, waiting to cross. Some looked my age, some older.

The big dude walked toward me smiling, like he knew me. Then he stuck out one of his big hands and said, "What's up little Battlefield? I'm Yancey Bettis. I was over at your house a few months ago at the meeting." I gave him a pound, and he squeezed my hand like it was a soggy sponge.

"Oh yeah, I remember. How you doing, sir?" I replied. "You're the one with the ranch in Nickelodeon, Kansas, right?"

"It's Nicodemus," he chuckled like a big NFL version of Santa Claus. "And you don't have to call me sir, little brotha. You can call me Big Bet like everyone else does."

"I'm sorry. It's just a habit . . . Mr. Big Bet." I replied.

"That's cool. It's a good habit to have. We just brought some of the fellas out here. A lot of them have never been to a game before, and this is a big one," Mr. Bettis said, as he waved at a couple of fans who recognized him from his playing days.

"So you guys brought all of the kids from the ranch?" I stood beneath his huge shadow while he signed a couple of autographs.

"Most of them. A few were lucky to be with their families over the holidays. The rest of them are here. The ranch is their family; I treat all of them like sons and brothers." Mr. Bettis smiled proudly.

"That's awesome, Mr. Bett—I meant Big Bet."

"There you go! You got it! I'm headed over to the tent to stuff my gut. See you in the game, Little Battlefield." Mr. Bettis gave me another knuckle crackling pound and joined the rest of the tailgating crew.

I was still on the curb waiting to cross the street when about thirteen of the boys from Mr. Bettis's ranch passed me. They all looked cool; nobody meanmugged me. Two even said, 'what's up'.

After a taxi and two loaded fan buses shuttled by, the crosswalk was all clear. If I didn't go then, I'd be standing on the curve all afternoon. When the last bus finally passed, I looked to the other side of the street. I dropped my dad's keys, bent over to pick them up, and tied my shoes while I was down there. What I saw when I looked up again, would've been the first scene in a bad nightmare three months ago.

Tariq Molten was standing on the other side of the street, alone, with one foot on the crosswalk. I've never seen ghosts before, but that's what it felt like.

I stood up, took a deep breath, stared straight ahead, and then made my way across. Tariq tugged on his gloves at the wrist, zipped his coat up all the way, and headed straight for me. He looked at me like *I* was the ghost, like he never thought he'd see my face again.

I wasn't scared. For those three months, I thought more about how being at the ranch would change his life. And not one day did I worry about facing the wrath of Tariq Molten.

We held up traffic as we faced off in the middle of the street. Cars honked, and brakes screeched to a halt, but we just stood there with our heads up high. Neither one of us blinked or backed down.

But something was different this time around. I could feel it. Tariq didn't mean-mug me. He didn't ball up his fists. He didn't grit his teeth. The venom he had on his grill the last time I saw him was gone. I saw no revenge in his eyes.

He slid his right hand in his coat pocket. I didn't flinch nor did I jump. And instead of a gun, he pulled out a piece of folded paper. He handed it to me and then said in a clear, still voice, "This is yours. You know, just in case you forgot it. Don't worry, I made a copy."

I opened it up and he watched me read the whole thing. He could see the shock on my face, the disbelief in my eyes. It was the prayer I said for him in the hospital room; every single word that I desperately threw up to heaven was written down neatly.

Even though he was unconscious; somehow, he heard me.

For me, it wasn't so hard to believe that maybe, just maybe, he had another visitor at his bedside that night.

Creator . . . thank you.

I don't know how I got here or why you brought me here,

but thank you for sparing our lives this evening.

Tariq is no kin to me, neither is Pacino,

but I know in your eyes
that we could be brothers.

Everything that I pray for, in my life,
I ask you to pass along to Tariq, to Pacino:
To be loved, to be protected, to be given a chance at
a good life.

You know our hearts better than we could ever
know, Father
so I ask you, I beg of you,
give Tariq the kind of life that he deserves,
the kind of life that he probably dreamed for a long
time ago, but gave up on.

Renew his faith and let him know that you never,
ever give up on us.

And, Father, when he wakes up, and gets out of
this hospital bed,
let him know that there are people in this world
that care about him.

In your most righteous name I pray . . . Amen

About the Author

A native of Kansas City, MO, Derrick D. Barnes is a graduate of Jackson State University, where he earned a BA in marketing. He is the author of *Stop, Drop, and Chill* and *The Low-Down Bad-Day Blues*, two books for early readers. His YA novel, *The Making of Dr. Truelove,* was recognized by the American Library Association as a Quick Pick for Reluctant Readers. He is also the author of the popular chapter book series, *Ruby and the Booker Boys.* Prior to becoming a published author, Derrick wrote best-selling copy for Hallmark Cards and was the first African-American male staff writer for the company. The owner of Say Word Creative Communication, a copywriting company, Derrick also writes the popular blog, Raising the Mighty, which chronicles his experiences raising four beautiful Black boys in America. He resides in Charlotte, NC, with his wife, Dr. Tinka Barnes, and their four sons, Ezra, Solomon, Silas, and Nnamdi.